# Secret Desires

J.L. REGEN

*In loving memory of Cecile Cooper*

# Secret Desires

*Chapter One*

Margo Simmons gripped the edges of the leather chair. Devastated after receiving a letter about her Uncle Harry's death, she didn't know what to expect from Mr. Steinberg. Her only other encounter with lawyers had been during the reading of her father's will. Though she was only five at the time, she remembered her mother's anguish over losing her husband and becoming a single parent.

An older gentleman clothed in pinstripes walked into the office as she reflected on the past.

"I'm sorry your mother couldn't be here for the reading," the family lawyer said. "You've grown into a lovely young woman."

Margo blinked back tears at memories of good times shared with Uncle Harry. "Not so young. I'm twenty-three."

The portly man squeezed himself into a swivel chair and peered at her over wire-rimmed bifocals.

Margo gripped her knees to steady her nerves. "They're downsizing at her dress shop. She was afraid to leave early. My stepfather is furious because Uncle Harry didn't leave him any money."

Mr. Steinberg nodded in sympathy at the pained expression on the young woman's face. "It saddens me to hear Jerry hasn't changed.

However, since you're the only one present to hear your uncle's will, I'll get to the point. Harry has left you his Riverside Drive condominium and the sum of two hundred and fifty thousand dollars."

Margo jumped up from the chair and hugged the man. "This is a miracle. I can't wait to tell my Mom. She's wanted me to get out on my own. Now I can."

The attorney pushed bifocals up his fleshy nose. "In today's market, two hundred and fifty thousand dollars won't last long unless invested wisely."

The only thing Margo knew about investments was she didn't have enough money to make any.

"Mr. Steinberg, do you know of someone who can advise me so I make wise investments?"

He raised his hand. "Not so fast my dear. Your Uncle stipulated that you be gainfully employed for a year before you can claim your inheritance. The last time your mother and I spoke, you were studying to be a French teacher."

Margo stared at the vibrant red dragon design on an Oriental rug and thought of the threadbare one under her rickety dining room table. Her eyes darted from his monogrammed attaché case to her worn shoulder strap bag. She had to find a way to tell him of her predicament.

"I've been looking for a teaching job for a year, but I am on the substitute list and have a part-time job at a dry cleaner so I'm employed. I know it's not a professional job, but it's respectable work."

Mr. Steinberg made notes in her uncle's folder. "I'm afraid that won't do, my dear. Harry loved you but was very clear on the type of employment."

A tear rolled down Margo's cheek. "I don't know how much longer I can live at home. Mama is working twice as hard since Jerry was laid off from his job at the newspaper. He couldn't get the hang of technology. He's been on disability from an old back injury. Could I at least speak to an investment counsellor to get an idea of what to do with my inheritance? It would give me something to dream about."

Margo sat on her hands as she waited with trepidation for the lawyer's response. Since childhood, all she ever wanted was to be part of a happy family and not have to worry about money. Instead of granting her wishes, life had brought her a mean stepfather. Jerry fractured a childhood that had been filled with love when her birth father was alive.

Mr. Steinberg lifted a business card from a sterling silver box. "I highly recommend Edward Master. He's with the investment banking firm of Chartwell, Morgan, and Master. He'll give you solid advice. Shall I see if he's available now?"

Margo glanced at her watch. "Yes, but it's kind of short notice, isn't it?"

"Your uncle was my good friend. Let's see if Master is available." The attorney lifted the receiver and punched in a number. A few minutes later, he wrote an address on a slip of paper. "You're in luck, young lady. Mr. Master has an opening at eleven." He checked his watch. "It's now ten. It shouldn't take you an hour to walk from Grand Central to Fifty Ninth and Madison."

Steinberg handed her the paper. "Hurry along."

Margo stole a glance at her checkbook. She had exactly a hundred dollars.

"Mr. Steinberg, I don't have enough money for your fee until I get my next paycheck."

The lawyer extended his hand. "No worries. Harry loved you very much. He's taken care of the legal expenses. I feel like a brute treating you this way, but I must adhere to the terms of your uncle's will. Please keep me posted on your job status. The minute you've signed a full-time teaching contract, I will start the paperwork on your inheritance and condo title transfer."

Margo grasped the man's fingers. "Thanks so much for your help."

He smiled. "Say hello to your mother."

"Will do."

Margo retraced her steps to the elevator and headed for the subway line to take her to Mr. Master's office. She fantasized about taking a vacation in Italy. She could buy a new couch for the living room. The one she was sleeping on was overdue at the Salvation Army. It made her feel like a homeless person. Then there was the dress in Lord & Taylor's window her mother had admired. She'd hoped to do something to reward the woman for all she'd sacrificed to raise Margo with Jerry absent most of the time. She still needed to pay off her student loans, which were messing up her credit rating.

Life shouldn't be so complicated at twenty three. The secret desires she'd locked away in the hope chest of her heart would have to wait to be set free.

MARGO ARRIVED in Edward Master's Madison Avenue office a half hour early. The old money Ivy League environment made her feel uncomfortable. She buried her nose in the latest issue of the Education Journal.

Maybe this wasn't a good idea. She retraced her steps to the door.

Someone called her name. "Ms. Simmons?"

An attractive woman about Margo's age offered a cardboard smile. "Mr. Master will see you in his office."

Margo followed her down a long corridor. What had she done? Mr. Master was probably a stuffy older man who'd talk down to her like Jerry. She walked into a spacious office to gaze at a tall man with a head of thick, wavy black hair.

He dismissed the secretary and extended his right hand. "Edward Master."

His athletic body, firm jaw, and bedroom eyes mesmerized her. So much so she forgot the way his calloused fingers made her skin bristle when she shook his hand. This guy was hot and young. He reminded her of Mr. Manero, a history professor in her senior year of high school. He was dreamy. She'd looked forward to history class so she could stare at him.

Stop it. She scolded herself. She'd just been told Uncle Harry had passed away. Out of respect for the departed, she shouldn't indulge in sexual feelings. Margo couldn't help herself. She imagined those fingers exploring her body. She'd allow herself one more languorous look and switch her brain to business mode.

"Please have a seat," Master said, pointing to a chair in front of a mahogany desk filled with engraved crystal awards.

Margo sunk onto the plush leather and crossed her shapely legs.

"I'm sorry for your loss. From what Mr. Steinberg told me, your Uncle Harry was quite a man."

"I spent a lot of time with him after my birth father died. He was my favorite relative. I've never had enough money to invest so this will be a new experience. Mr. Steinberg said I can't tap into my inheritance until I find a full-time job. I hope it will happen soon."

Margo could feel her toes curling in her shoes as Master's dimples widened into a smile.

"First, call me Edward. Mr. Master is my grandfather. He founded this firm. I'm the conservative Vice President among my colleagues."

His voice was so sensuous. His stare intense.

First encounters usually didn't have this effect on Margo.

"Good to know, but can you give me an idea of what I should invest in?"

He handed her a pad. "It would help if you could write down how much you think you'll need to live on for the next two years. We can talk about how to invest the remaining sum."

"Sounds like a plan."

Margo made two columns. One was her wish list, filled with the designer clothes she admired every time she walked up Madison Avenue to meet her mother at The Store off Fifth, the small boutique where Diana worked as a seamstress. She added matching shoes and bags. The other, necessities of life, was for the basics of food, maintenance, and medical insurance.

Before handing the pad to Mr. Master, she crossed out her wish list.

"Seems you're conservative as well."

"I have to be with student loans to repay."

He turned a page in his agenda. "I'll do a preliminary profile. When can you come in to discuss it?"

Margo lost her focus. He was so handsome, but his type of guy probably only went out with girls from schools like Vassar.

He repeated the question. "Miss Simmons, did you hear me?"

She wanted to say tomorrow but wouldn't press her luck. "Friday is my early day. I could be here by five thirty if that's okay."

"Good enough. See you then. My secretary will show you out. Good luck with your job search."

"Thanks."

He extended his hand. This time it was warm and inviting. She noted the wedding band. Stop daydreaming.

# Chapter Two

Edward fingered his wedding band. At quitting time he hated the thought of going home to an empty house. He stopped into a pizza place, grabbed a soda, and walked home. Opening the front door of his Sutton Place townhouse, he stepped into an empty, cavernous space. He tired of eating alone with only the sound of his voice for company. When Annabelle, his wife of ten years, was alive, he was happy to be there.

In the year since her death, it had become a place to admire art work from their vacations. People visited museums. They didn't live in them. He remembered a time when laughter and music filled each room. Annabelle gave the best parties in town. Her vivacious personality was hard to resist. All traces that a real family lived here had vanished with her passing.

As he climbed up the stairs to the master bedroom, Edward stopped short of the door. At thirty-three, his life was meaningless.

He avoided the king-sized bed where he'd made love to Annabelle and opened a cavernous walk-in closet to finger dresses and gowns. A year ago, they'd been worn by his wife. Now, they were remnants of a life snuffed out too soon at thirty.

Edward's hand fell on Annabelle's favorite, a Dior lavender lace creation. He smiled at the memory of how he'd removed it after their first anniversary party. He'd worked the delicate zipper and buttons to free her from the material. As the gown slipped off her silky shoulders, he'd carried her onto the bed for a night of passion.

He held the silky material to his nose to sniff the lingering essence of her favorite fragrance, Chanel No. 5. He'd never be able to smell it on her again. Unable to part with it, Edward returned the gown to the closet.

He heard footsteps in the hallway. He so wished they were Annabelle's, there to greet him after a long day at work and caress away cares of the day. Regrettably, his housekeeper appeared in the doorway.

"Sir, is there anything else you need before I leave for the evening?" Emma asked.

"Can you help me put these clothes into a garment bag?"

"Of course."

Halfway out of the bedroom, Edward turned around and placed the clothes back on the rack. He held the garment bag against his cheek. "These are all I have left of her."

Edward saw the look of sorrow on Emma's face.

"Begging your pardon, sir, but Mrs. Master has been gone a year. It's time to let someone else use these clothes."

Swept up in the aura of his wife, Edward could only nod. "You're right. Tomorrow morning, I'll have Roger take me to the dry cleaner to have them readied for new owners."

"See you then, sir."

He dreaded another night in the house alone. "Wait, could we talk for a while?"

Emma shook her head. "Sorry sir, any other time, but tonight I must get home to help Jeremy with his homework."

"Of course. How is Danny?"

She laughed. "Ten going on twenty."

"They're fun at that age. Thank you for your help. Enjoy being with your son."

Edward heard the door close. He pushed back the curtains to watch

Emma walk down the street. He shouldn't be bothering people with his problems. The loss of appetite wasn't as bad as the sleepless nights. After a year, he still woke up at midnight expecting Annabelle to appear in the bedroom doorway. In his mind, he knew she was gone forever, but his heart ached for the closeness.

He dragged his attaché case in a hand that longed to reach out to someone. He'd work until sleep overcame him. On the way to his office, he peeked into the guest room he and Annabelle had planned to turn into a nursery. It was as barren as his life.

The numbers on the savings plan the Simmons woman gave him began to blur. He rested his glasses and went into the guest room. Since Annabelle's passing, Edward couldn't bear to sleep in their bed alone.

Margo hurried along the street to her Bronx apartment building. After sitting in the patrician law firm, she almost hated to enter the dreary lobby with peeling orange and brown wallpaper and a broken intercom system.

She pressed the elevator button and waited several minutes. "Darn, out of order again."

As she walked up eight flights of stairs, Margo reached into her bag for keys. In a hurry to get to work, she'd left them on her bedroom dresser. She knocked on the door several times before her mother opened.

Diana Simmons's eyes and nose were red. Her mouth drooped.

Margo dropped her bag and reached for her mother. "What's wrong?"

"I had a rough day at work. We're short staffed, and the boss is stressed so she took it out on me. Jerry is irritating me. Ignore whatever he says."

Margo led her mother to a lumpy, faded green couch. Bought in a thrift shop, it creaked when they sat down.

"I spoke to Mr. Steinberg this morning. Uncle Harry left me the condo and money, but I can't claim either until I have a full-time professional position."

Her mother's shoulders slumped. "He was a good man. You should get away and have a happy life. How much money?"

"Two hundred and fifty thousand dollars. I just came from the investment banker Mr. Steinberg recommended. He's going to help me grow my inheritance."

"Be careful how you use it. You're too picky. Sometimes you have to settle for whatever school has an opening. Young people today have no sense of responsibility," Jerry Simmons said, listening as he sat on the edge of the couch.

Margo ignored the man's sarcasm. "I value money too much to waste a penny."

Jerry moved to a rocking chair across from them.

Margo looked at the food stains on his t-shirt and the hole in his sock.

"You won't waste a penny of your uncle's money, but I gave you a roof over your head through four years of college. So you should reimburse me once you can claim your inheritance."

Diana shook her fist. "Leave the girl alone. Besides, you couldn't fill one of Harry's shoes."

Jerry pointed a finger at his wife. "When we got married, you told me your brother would help us out. You lied to me."

He turned his head in Margo's direction. "Now, we're stuck with her. If I'd known the way things would turn out when we got hitched, I'd have backed out. The kid isn't even my blood."

Diana placed her head in her hands and cried. "It's not my fault my beloved Alex died of a heart attack. Do you always have to say mean things in front of Margo? She's been through so much."

She kissed Margo's forehead. "I've lost my appetite. My feet are killing me. I'm taking a shower and going to bed. I fixed a plate for you."

Jerry shook his head. "What about me?"

Margo walked toward her bedroom.

Then she turned to face her stepfather. "I paid for my education with student loans. As to the rest, what would you have me do as a child? Take in laundry? I don't owe you anything. You owe my mother respect."

Margo pointed to the kitchen. "You can have what Mom left for me. I've lost my appetite."

Jerry smirked. "Don't mind if I do."

Margo missed her real father. Sometimes she wished she'd never been born. Jerry was a sorry excuse for a husband. A smooth operator, he'd taken advantage of her mother for too long. It was time for things to change for her and Diana. She had to get a teaching job if only to prove Jerry was wrong about her. Then again, he'd never taken the time to get to know her as a child or an adult.

MARGO TURNED on her computer and searched for teaching jobs, hoping one of the countless schools she'd applied to had responded.

"Darn, nothing," she mumbled.

Her room was stifling. She turned on the ceiling fan and walked down the hall to the bathroom. Leaving the door open to ventilate, she stepped into the shower. Friday couldn't come fast enough.

As her head hit the pillow, Margo closed her eyes and dreamed of opening her first savings account and Edward Master's dreamy smile

# Chapter Three

U p before the alarm went off, Edward stepped into the suit he'd selected the night before. He'd given Annabelle's jewelry to her parents but didn't know if he'd have the strength to part with her gowns. He walked into the eat-in kitchen with a sour stomach.

"Good morning, Emma."

He took a mouthful of a poached egg and a few sips of coffee she'd prepared and returned to the bedroom closet. Lifting Annabelle's gowns into his arms, he headed out. The hole in his heart grew bigger with each step he took down the staircase and out the front door. It wasn't fair to lose her at thirty.

"Let me help you, Mr. M," Roger, the family driver, said, holding the door open as Edward placed the bags on the back seat of the Mercedes.

"You're doing the right thing, sir. Mrs. M will always be in your heart."

Edward slid next to the garment bags.

"What's the plan, sir?"

"I'll have them cleaned and donated to Cancer Care."

A few minutes later, Roger parked curbside of Fong's Dry Cleaner on Fifty Seventh and First Avenue.

Edward began to have second thoughts. "Maybe I'm being too hasty."

"Sir, you did everything humanly possible to prolong Mrs. Master's life. Now let someone else enjoy wearing those gowns."

Edward lifted the bags into his arms. "I'll call when I need you Roger, thank you."

~

THE STORE WAS CROWDED.

Edward rested the garment bags on an empty chair and took his place on line. While waiting his turn, Edward took stock of his life. He was Vice President in the firm of Chartwell, Morgan, and Master. Started by the grandfathers of all three men, it had withstood the tests of time and economic turbulence. In between Choate Rosemary Hall and Harvard, he spent summers building houses with Habitat for Humanity. Looking back on that experience, he missed the camaraderie. The work gave purpose and meaning to his life. He'd always championed the underdog and seeing struggling families move into new homes was rewarding.

While Edward attended Harvard Business School for his MBA, Grandfather Master acknowledged his sweat and toil by bequeathing to Edward the family yacht, The Outrigger. A lifelong love affair with boating began. He didn't relish steering it alone.

Edward startled when he realized the girl behind the counter was Margo Simmons, his new client. He'd been wrong about her hair color. She stood a few inches shorter than his six feet, and her blonde hair stopped at the shoulders. Sapphire eyes, not to mention full, sensuous lips mesmerized him. She had a nice way about her and handled customers well, especially the man in front of him.

"How long does it take to iron a shirt? I have to get to work."

"If you'll give me another minute, I'll see what's going on."

"You bet you will," the annoyed customer said in a snarly tone.

Edward frowned at the man's rudeness. "Come on, give the girl a break. She's doing her best."

The man scrunched up his face. "Butt out."

"Did you forget your manners? You're talking to a lady."

Margo returned a few seconds later. "Here you are, sir. Light starch around the collars."

The irate man paid the bill, grabbed the package out of her hands, and slammed the door.

Edward stepped up to the counter. "Sorry that guy was so rude. You have a lot of patience."

She tried to act nonchalant, took his garments, and gave him a ticket. "I have to. I want to teach elementary school kids. By the way, nice to see you again."

"You too. Which college?"

"Hunter. I went part-time for six years. I was told substitute teaching is a good way to get a foot in the door, but the list is so long."

Edward waited off to the side as Margo helped another customer. While the tailor followed her into a dressing room, Margo talked to the customer's little girl.

"Hi, Daisy."

"Hello, Miss Malgo." She covered her mouth and rolled her big eyes. "So sorry. I mess up your name."

"Don't worry, my little friend. It's hard for Japanese students to say certain letters. I studied your language. You should hear how funny I sounded."

She handed the girl a lollipop. "A reward for trying."

The child ran under the counter and gave Margo a big hug. "I miss you when we return to Tokyo."

"Me too. What did you learn in day care today?"

Daisy sang a song.

Edward clapped at the end. "You're a very talented young lady."

Daisy blushed and went running to join her mother in the dressing room.

Mrs. Miyoki came out and turned to Margo. "Thank you so much for watching my little one."

"The pleasure was all mine."

The interaction between Margo and the youngster made Edward

realize how lonely he was. He moved up to the counter. "They're cute at that age."

"Someday I want one just like her. What a little munchkin."

He reached into his wallet for a business card and scribbled his cell phone number on the back. "I don't remember giving you my card."

Margo dropped it into her jeans pocket and motioned for him to come closer. She whispered in his ear. "Sorry I can't talk longer."

Her cheek brushed against his face. He was surprised and confused to feel attraction for another woman, especially one much younger.

"See you on Friday," Edward said, widening the smile on his face.

ON HER BREAK, Margo took a closer look at Edward's business card. Black script on ivory stock, work number, email, and the title Vice President. The card was as eye-catching as the man. She secured it in her wallet, remembering the scent of his cologne and the way she'd boldly leaned into him. If there hadn't been customers in the shop, she'd have kissed him.

Then she recalled his wedding ring. All the good ones were taken.

# Chapter Four

When Margo turned to cover a garment in plastic, Mr. Fong was beside her.

"Mr. Master is a good man," he said. "He's been a loyal customer for over a decade. His wife passed away last June. This is the first time I've seen him in the store. So sad to be all alone in the world. I hope you took good care of him."

Margo frowned. "Of course I help everyone. That's my job."

A ringing counter bell interrupted her next thought. "Yes, sir, how may I help you?"

A plump man dropped a pile of clothing onto the counter. "I need these slacks tomorrow and the jacket on Friday."

Margo separated the garments and tagged each of them.

He winked. "I've been watching you, honey. You're so organized."

Margo cringed when he squeezed her arm and patted her hand.

He leaned in closer. "I could use someone like you in my office. You know, to organize me."

Mr. Fong moved away from the register and next to Margo. "Take your clothes elsewhere. We don't want them here."

"Up yours," he said, giving Mr. Fong the finger before leaving.

Her insides were shaking. Nothing had happened, but she still felt violated.

Margo had started office work at sixteen. She'd scrimped and saved ever since, yet only had enough money in her checking account to get back and forth to school and the dry cleaner.

She glanced at a huge wall clock. In another hour, she'd head over to her mother's workplace, The Store off Fifth, a lady's specialty boutique around the corner and down the block from Bergdorf's. Like her daughter, Diana didn't have it easy, laboring in the store six days a week to pick up the slack from Jerry's long stretches of unemployment. Margo hoped her mother didn't lose her job. As much as she loved her, she wanted a place and life of her own, free of her stepfather's comments about her credit cards or why, at twenty three, she was often home so late. Her inheritance couldn't buy happiness. She wanted a partner. Did she dare to think about Edward Master? Maybe, then again, they came from two different worlds.

Margo clocked out and put the Closed sign on the front door. It was a sunny June day, pretty enough to inspire an artist to paint a landscape. She took the long way to the subway, thinking of Edward's smile as she walked and wondering if she could work up the courage to flirt with him now that she knew he was single.

# Chapter Five

On Friday Margo left the store early, giving herself ample time to arrive at Edward's office. She hoped she'd be able to keep her mind on the investment advice he'd give her. The mere sound of his voice on the phone made her think about what it would be like to be intimate with him.

Margo stepped into an open elevator and pressed the button for Edward's floor.

Abigail, his secretary, greeted her in the reception area. "Hi, Mr. Master is waiting for you."

"Thank you."

Naughty thoughts went through Margo's mind. Nice and easy does it.

She took the same seat in his office as her last visit and held onto her knees to keep them from knocking together.

As Edward explained a mix of certificates of deposit and other investment choices, Margo marveled at the man's grasp of the subject matter. A mouthwatering body and brains in one fine specimen of a man.

"I hope I haven't overwhelmed you. Look over what's in the portfolio. We can set up another meeting to discuss whatever you don't understand."

Every so often Margo felt him staring at her. "You know your finances. I hope I do half as well as a teacher."

Edward moved into an empty chair next to her. "I saw the way you were with that little girl in the dry cleaner. You're a natural with kids."

Margo smiled. His nearness sent tremors through her body.

She shifted her weight on the chair and saw Edward steal a glance at her legs. His eyes lingered on them a moment.

She took off her blazer and draped it around the back of the chair.

"I'm sure things will change for the better once you're a teacher."

She frowned. "Every day when I get home from work, I check my emails. Rejection after rejection. I'm beginning to wonder if I'll ever have a classroom of my own."

Edward rose from his seat and walked her to the doorway. "You will. You're a determined woman, Margo Simmons. Be confident in what you have to offer to students."

"I won't stop until I reach my goal, but I would like someone waiting for me at the finish line."

Edward smiled. "I'll do my best to help you with your finances."

"Thanks. It would help if at least one thing in my life was improving."

Margo saw Abigail waiting outside the door to escort her to the reception area. She had to do something to let Edward know how she felt. Making a slow turn, she walked back to where he was standing and kissed his cheek. "Just because."

*With one look, Edward had rocked my world.* So much so she almost went into Bergdorf's instead of her mother's shop. Retracing her steps, she headed for The Store off Fifth and walked to the back to find her mother hunched over a sewing machine.

She admired a silver lame sheath dangling from a hanger. "Another occasion for Mrs. Jolie?"

Mrs. Simmons nodded. "Yes, we talk as I work on her alterations. For all her wealth, I think the thing she wanted most was a child. She seems so sad and withdrawn lately."

"There you go. What did you always tell me? Nothing in life is perfect. Here's a woman with tons of money, and she's unhappy."

Diana shook her head. "Look at these pantsuits. The money she wastes on little things like missing buttons. She could sew them on herself. I should be spending more time tailoring that cruise line and those leisure outfits, but we're known for the personal touch."

Margo worried about the dark circles under her mother's eyes. "Why don't you call it a day? You look exhausted."

"I am, but I have another hour to go before I can leave. I can't lose this job," Diana said, craning her neck. "Do something meaningful with your life. Are you sure teaching is what you want?"

"I've dreamed of it since I was a kid."

"You were adorable. I remember when we had the house on Long Island before your father died. You'd pretend teach at a makeshift blackboard in the basement."

"I want to help children, Mom."

"I know how much you want a job, but don't let it drive you crazy."

"Let me help you clean up. I'm glad this is my last Saturday working in the shop. I can devote more time over the summer to a job search."

~

THE NEXT DAY, Margo arrived at work to find the firemen exiting the dry cleaner.

Mr. Fong stood inside the doorway, hands on his hips. "Cheap landlord never fixed the wiring. I hope that between the building owner's insurance and my insurance it will cover the losses."

"With luck, if the Fire Marshals do find the cause was the wiring, the building owner will be obligated to cover your losses." Margo said hoping it would bolster Mr. Fongs morale.

Margo helped him sort through whatever hadn't been smoke-damaged or charred.

"Ouch," she said, rubbing her shoulder.

"Are you okay, Ms. Margo?"

"Yes, Mr. Fong. I pulled a muscle. I have to be more careful the way I lift large bundles of clothing."

"Why don't you call it a day and go home. I can manage."

EXHAUSTED by the time she reached her apartment, Margo turned on the ceiling fan in her room to keep from fainting from an onslaught of early summer heat.

She reached for her cell phone and texted her best friend, Nancy.

*The cleaners where I work had an electrical fire*

Nancy called her right back. "What is Mr. Fong going to do?"

"He is borrowing space a few blocks away. I know the place. It won't be great working conditions, but I can't give notice until I have another job."

"Tell me about it," Nancy said. "I audition all week long and then wait on tables on the weekends. How's Sergio?"

"Dumped that jerk. My love life's as empty; I might as well become a nun."

Margo didn't want to jinx things. She'd tell Nancy about Edward once she knew if it would go anywhere.

Nancy and Margo had been best friends since grade school, but her taste in guys hadn't changed since their teen years. Margo had graduated from the school of dating bad boys like Sergio and wasn't about to enroll again.

"Have to run. Talk to you later."

DIANA HAD BEEN PUTTING in a ton of overtime for the last three months and grabbing fast food. Margo wanted to do something nice for her tonight. She gathered utensils and ingredients for a nutritious dinner, wishing she would be looking at Edward across the table. When Diana came home from the store and heard what happened at the dry cleaner, she forced a smile. "All that matters is your safety."

She answered a ringing house phone. "Hello? Who is calling please? Hold on, I'll see if she's home."

Diana covered the mouthpiece and gave Margo a cautious look. "Sergio wants to speak to you."

"Thanks, Mom. I'll take it in the bedroom."

Margo carried the cordless phone and plopped down on the bed.

"How's it going?" her former boyfriend asked.

"Working all the time."

"I remember you had your heart set on teaching little kids."

"Still do."

Margo wondered why he was calling her. They'd had a big fight over his not wanting to go to college and had broken up more than a year ago.

"I've been thinking about you a lot. I feel like a jerk for the way I acted on our last date."

"Did you have amnesia?"

"Okay, it's been a while. Now that I'm on board, my uncle's auto repair store is doing well. The money is good, and I'm bringing in lots of business. We're branching out to limo service."

"Glad to hear you're more settled."

"Look, Margo. We had something good in high school. Can we meet for coffee?"

"Why?"

"Because I liked being with you, and I'm hoping you don't hate me so much you won't see me for an hour."

Maybe he'd changed. "Okay, but only for a little while."

"Great."

"There's a coffee shop a block from Hunter at Sixty-Eighth and Lexington. Let's meet there tomorrow at nine for a light breakfast. Then, I can spend the rest of the morning in the college library doing more research for my job hunt."

"See you then."

Margo walked back to the living room where Diana was knitting.

She saw the worried look on her mother's face. "I'm not going to do anything stupid."

"I said the same thing to my mother. I was married at seventeen, pregnant at eighteen, and divorced at twenty-three."

"Mom, Sergio was my first love. I emphasize the word was. It's over for me."

Then, why see him again?

"We parted with anger. I don't want to carry that with me anymore."

Margo inserted a romance movie into the DVD. "For two hours, we're going to escape."

"Great timing. Jerry is out bowling with his buddies."

During the love scenes, Margo closed her eyes and imagined someone special holding her in his arms. She was older and wiser now and not about to give her heart to a dreamer or, as Grandmother used to say, "A man with champagne taste on a beer budget."

SUNDAY MORNING while walking to the coffee shop from the subway, Margo had second thoughts about her meeting with Sergio. All of her life she'd done the right thing. She'd seen what happened to girls who'd gotten pregnant. Some had to return home to live with their parents and work in menial jobs to make ends meet with no hope of it ever changing. Margo wouldn't let that happen to her. She wouldn't settle for a smooth talker with a handsome face. She'd make her education pay off and if she didn't meet Mr. Right for her, she'd adopt and give her son or daughter the kind of home life she'd always desired.

In the past when she'd met Sergio, Margo made sure her makeup was perfect. Today, instinct told her to forego the lipstick and wear her hair pulled back in a ponytail. The first to arrive, she took a seat in the front booth of the coffee shop and waited.

"Hi, Margo, long time no see," said Sam, the owner.

"I've been working, Sam."

"You're a breath of fresh air. Most of the kids who come in here drop out."

"I agree," Sergio said.

Margo looked up to see her former boyfriend sliding into the seat opposite her.

She studied his face. Laugh lines bordered his eyes. His curly hair had lost its luster, but the boyish charm was still there.

He reached for her hand.

She pulled back.

Sam placed two menus on the table. "Take your time."

Sergio smiled. "So, how've you been?"

"Fine."

"Your hair is longer now."

Margo pulled on a stray strand.

"You've gotten prettier."

If that remark was supposed to win points, it wasn't happening.

Sam returned. "What will it be, folks?"

"I'm not very hungry. A toasted English muffin and tea, please," Margo said.

"Make mine a ham omelet with home fries, buttered toast and a cup of java."

Margo looked at the grease under Sergio's fingertips. In the past, he'd always made her feel comfortable, like stepping into warm slippers. The way he looked at her made her feel cheap. She began to fidget.

He reached for her hand once more. "I really do want to take you out."

She pulled back. "On our last date, you fought with a waiter in a restaurant."

"He accused me of cheating him out of a tip," Sergio said through clenched teeth.

Margo shook her finger. "You pulled out a knife. Your temper is going to get you killed."

"Can I take you out for a belated graduation celebration? We can double date, if you like. I know this cool hall that does small parties."

"I graduated more than a year ago."

Sergio threw his hands in the air. "Well, I guess that's it."

Sam brought their food. "Enjoy kids."

Margo ate a mouthful and rested her fork. "There's no point to this. I should leave."

She headed to the library, disappointed that Sergio hadn't changed. They'd had good times. However, she had grown up and wanted more than a physical relationship. He was still an overgrown kid. She wanted a man with who was mature in his outlook and had a heart, a mind, and a soul. She thought of Edward. He had a great mind, but remembering what Mr. Fong told her about his late wife, she wondered if his heart was had healed sufficiently to open up to someone new.

*Chapter Six*

Edward dreaded weekends, especially Sunday. He and Annabelle used to discuss the latest cultural happenings and world events in The New York Times, play a few rounds of tennis, and cuddle on the couch watching old movies. Since her passing, he'd become a workaholic, only breaking on Saturday morning to go to his health club. He was one of those guys that unless he could do something with someone he loved, he just did nothing.

His older sister Valeria constantly badgered him to find someone. In her case it meant fixing him up with one of her younger girl friends. When she started up on this theme he would cut her off at the knees and tell her to butt out of his personal life. In reality Annabelle did become one of her girlfriends and they were thick as thieves.

Dinner for one was depressing. Closing off the dining room, he ate on the kitchen counter. It was always a quick meal just to satisfy the bodies' basic needs. Put whatever Emma left for him into the microwave, pour himself a glass of ice tea and he was done with dinner in fifteen minutes. Top it off with a double expresso from the Krupp coffee machine he and Annabelle got as a wedding present and he was ready to return to work in his home office.

They'd only just met, but he thought about Margo. She reminded him of Annabelle when they first dated. Margo struck him as having the same independent nature and determination. Since Annabelle's death, all of the introductions from well-meaning friends were cookie cutter perfect women with the right stuff, except for a heart and a mind. He could tell Margo was different. She had both and a great body. With those curves, she could be a model.

Exhaustion forced his pen to drop. He turned off his computer and walked up to the bedroom. He still couldn't go in there. Loss and loneliness overwhelmed him. Turning around, he carried a novel down to the den, hoping sleep would come easier. More often than not he would fall asleep on the den sofa only to wake up the following morning with a backache.

Margo came to mind once more. She was a person in need, and he needed to be needed.

# Chapter Seven

Margo hated Monday. Everyone came into the store with a long face. At least they didn't have to sort through dirty laundry and spend most of their free time surfing the Internet looking for jobs.

During her break, she went out for a walk and bought some Diet Coke hoping the caffeine would get her through the afternoon. Every muscle in her body ached. At quitting time, she didn't even say good-night to Mr. Fong. Exhausted, she headed for home.

As the subway car travelled to the Bronx, Margo scrolled to Sergio's name in her contacts list and hit call.

He answered in one ring "How's it going? Did you change your mind?"

"I hope you have a lot of success with your business. I've given it a lot of thought, it's over between us." She turned off her phone before he could respond. Then she proceeded to delete his number from her phone.

Weary from transferring clothes to the temporary work location and adjusting to a new environment, Margo popped a frozen dinner in the microwave. When the timer went off, she carried it into the living room. About to sit on the couch, she heard Jerry snoring. He retreated here whenever he and Diana had a fight, which was now a weekly occurrence.

Margo went to her bedroom to look for jobs online.

To her surprise, Edward Master was her first customer the next morning. He looked around the new spot. "What happened to the other location?"

Margo brushed back strands of hair. "We had an electrical fire which damaged a lot of clothing."

He handed her a tuxedo. "That's too bad. I'm glad Mr. Fong found another place so quickly. I spilled something on the jacket. I have to go to a benefit at Lincoln Center. Can you include it with my other garments?"

Margo tagged it and handed him a receipt. "No problem. I love outdoor concerts and dancing in the summer.

I haven't been in a while. It's no fun without a partner. There is a great deal to be said for enjoying something through someone else's eyes."

Margo held her breath. *Please ask me out.*

"One is a lonely number. After our meeting, would you join me for dinner on Friday? The Versailles Restaurant is close by the office. They make fantastic calves liver with pearl onions in a wonderful tasting sauce."

She blushed a bit, thinking about gazing at him over candlelight at the restaurant. "I'd love to."

Maybe once they'd had some real conversation, Edward would relax. "Then, it's a date?"

Already he seemed a little looser. His shoulders dropped a bit, he almost smiled.

"Yes."

Chapter Eight

E dward walked out of the dry cleaner with a bounce in his stride. It would be nice to have a conversation with someone other than himself, especially when the person was as pretty as Margo.

He refocused his mind on business. An early riser, he liked to get into the office by seven thirty so he could read the Wall Street Journal, check his emails, and address client priorities before the phones started ringing.

His intercom beeped. "Sir, there's a long distance call from the headhunter in London on line two."

"Put him on."

"Mr. Master," the woman said. "I think I've found the perfect candidate to head the M&A Division of your New York office. He worked on Wall Street earlier in his career and has a solid background in international finance. He's available to speak with you tomorrow afternoon."

"Fine, the sooner I have someone in place, the better. See if he can be at my office at one thirty."

Edward logged in the appointment on his Outlook calendar. Margo's banter with the little Japanese girl came to mind. He opened an online folder on a new client the firm had recently acquired. A tire manufacturer in Asia was expanding operations into the States and in need of advice on the best way to make the plans happen with the greatest tax advantage. He'd set him up with the partner specializing in international tax law.

If only affairs of the heart were as easy to resolve as business problems. Edward had done his best to keep Annabelle alive, but there was that nagging doubt. Maybe if he'd tried the clinic in Zurich, they could've saved her.

Chapter Nine

Margo didn't like to ask for favors, but on Friday morning she summoned the courage with Mr. Fong. "Is it okay if I leave an hour earlier?"

She knew he'd say yes but wanted to give him the courtesy of a response.

"Sure. You're a good worker. Oh, by the way, it sounds like we'll be in this location for a while. The insurance company is giving me a hard time on our claim."

She nodded but was too excited to dwell on work stuff. She'd be seeing Edward soon. She couldn't think of anything else.

Margo hurried into the small bathroom to change into the outfit she'd hung in the closet. She thought of Edward's soft brown eyes framed by long eyelashes, a Brad Pitt smile, and broad shoulders. It might take a bit of doing to bring down the walls guarding his heart.

Margo snapped out of her daydream. If she didn't hurry, she'd be late. She called her mother in the store. "Mom, I have a date. I won't be home for dinner."

She could hear Diana's enthusiasm. "Wonderful."

"Hold on, dear. Jerry is on the other line."

Her mother's voice changed when she came back.

"Mama, are you okay?"

"Jerry called to say he's going to the gym with the guys Good that means I can enjoy a quiet evening. Lately, all we do is argue anyway. I'm so sorry to subject you to this constant bickering. Make something of your life. Enjoy your date. I have to finish hemming a gown."

Margo's heart sank. From the minute she met Jerry, she knew there would be trouble in the house. He wasn't like Papa. Her real father was a kind man who could brush away her bad dreams with the touch of his hand on her cheek. He cared about people.

She recalled a cold winter when she was four. Mrs. Hamilton, a senior with a bad hip, was having trouble balancing on her cane. Her father lifted the woman into his arms and handed her small bag of groceries to Margo as they travelled the four blocks home. Tempted to call off her date with Edward and keep her mother company, she changed her mind. Mama wasn't the type who looked for sympathy. Unlike Jerry, Diana wanted Margo to be happy.

MARGO FOLLOWED the receptionist past row on row of windowed offices in Edward's company. The Lucite and chrome furniture, floral arrangements in oversized vases, and patrician appearance of staff were impressive. At the end of the long hallway, she entered Edward's office. On her previous visit, she hadn't noticed the copies of Impressionist paintings and the book shelves lining three sides of the room.

His greeting was stiff and formal. "Hi. Good to see you again."

Edward closed the door and pointed to a small, leather couch. "I think we'll be more comfortable over there."

Margo watched him rub his neck. He seemed stressed. The way her luck was running, he'd cancel out. She would've loved to have massaged away his pain.

"We're opening an office in London. I've been poring over financial documents and leasing arrangements all day. I need to stretch my legs."

She relaxed a little bit. Good, they were still on for dinner.

"I know the feeling. I spoke to the realtor handling my late uncle's apartment. He left it to me in his will. I took one real estate course in college. It's so complicated. I can only imagine the kind of transactions in the corporate world and high-end commercial residences."

"See?" he said. "You're catching on to the lingo."

Edward was loosening up, which made him even more attractive to Margo. During a pause in the conversation, she lingered on his muscular body. He must work out a lot. Edward seemed the type who chose his clothes with attention to detail. The tie matched the shirt, and the socks matched the slacks. The initials on his cufflinks were the same as in his tie tack. His thick, black wavy hair was cut to a conservative length. She guessed a five o'clock shadow made frequent shaves a necessity in his line of work

His face was the best part. Prominent cheekbones and a high forehead showed little signs of wear for a man who'd survived the rigors of what she surmised to be Ivy League schools and the loss of his wife. She longed for a kiss.

Edward opened a leather-bound portfolio and handed Margo a printout. The numbers might as well have been hieroglyphics.

"I hope you don't think me simple-minded, but I could use your expertise here."

"Certainly."

Edward moved closer.

Heat rose in Margo's body as his hand brushed against her skirt.

He pointed to three columns on the page—Safe but Long-term, Medium Risk but Faster Return, and Fastest but Possibility of Rapid Market Change which could cause loss of principal. "I've listed the amounts of money that will bring you the greatest returns in each of these categories."

"I really appreciate this."

Margo thought of Jerry's sarcastic remarks. She had to get a teaching job, even if it meant settling. With full-time work, she could manage expenses on her uncle's condo. She'd convince her mother to divorce her stepfather and move in with her.

"I'll never give up on my teaching goals, but dreams won't pay the bills. You've given me a lot of advice for free. We can just go out for a drink if you're too tired for dinner."

Edward gave her a yearning look. She stared into his bright and intense eyes. *Take me right now, please.*

"Margo, I'm a widower with no children. The job and this firm will be here long after I cease to exist. It would give me pleasure to take you to dinner and talk about something other than business."

He glanced at his watch. "If we move along, we'll catch the tail end of one of the best piano players in town."

"Sounds good to me."

Margo's heart did somersaults. She wanted to spend more time with him. To get to know him.

He rose from the seat and slipped on his suit jacket. "Shall we?"

She loved looking at his taut body. As they walked to the door, she stammered. "Sure, I mean, yes."

MARGO RECALLED SEEING pictures of the Versailles Restaurant online. It was a miniature version of the famed palace outside of Paris.

They walked into a spacious room filled with velvet-lined banquettes beyond which extended a circular dining room. A crystal vase filled with fresh-cut, multicolored roses graced each table.

The maître d' shook his hand. "Good evening, Mr. Master. Nice to see you, it's been a while."

Edward pointed to a quiet table across from the bar. "We'll take that one, Henri."

"Bien sur, of course."

Henri took their beverage order, which Margo gave in French.

"I'm impressed," Edward said.

"I don't get to speak my favorite language often enough."

"I grew to love it and the country through my wife." He cleared his throat, looking awkward for a moment.

Margo remembered how she felt when her mother told her that her father wasn't coming back. A five-year-old couldn't offer much more than a hug. Then her uncle came to mind and with it the pain of remembrance.

Henri brought their drinks.

"Loss is hard. I still can't believe Uncle Harry is gone. He became like a father to me after my birth one died. We'd go to Central Park when I was a kid. He bought me my first bike. Then my aunt died, and he turned into a workaholic. I wish I could've spent more time with him when he was sick, but we lost contact."

Edward leaned toward her. "Let's focus on the present and enjoy dinner."

Margo sensed he might not want to deal with loss. She felt bad for elaborating. She hoped Edward took note of the way her short skirt rode upward when she sat revealing a great deal of thigh and the blouse that clung to the curves of her body. It had been a while since she'd enjoyed dressing for a man.

A waiter handed them menus.

Margo gulped at the prices. She hadn't seen such numbers since Uncle Harry treated her to dinner for her sixteenth birthday at the Waldorf Astoria.

Edward loosened his tie and craned his neck.

"Still hurts?"

"It will pass. What do you do when you're not at work?"

Margo took out a small, digital camera. "I love photography. This is a toy, but I keep it handy in case I see something I want to shoot. The Nikon, a gift from my uncle, is at home. When I have a camera in my hand, I feel free. It's become more of a passion each year."

The waiter came. Salivating for half the items on the menu, Margo chose a simple salad and veal entrée.

She bit down on a breadstick. "How about you, Edward?"

"Sailing, the thrill of speeding to the finish line in yacht races. I tried water skiing. I lost my balance a few times, but it was a lot of fun."

"Where have you sailed?"

"Bermuda is my favorite. I think you'd like it there."

"I've heard about the pink sand. I hate the thought of winter coming. If it's anything like the last one, I may head south for winter. I'm sure they have teaching jobs in Florida."

Their entrees arrived. Margo took a mouthful. "Delicious."

He reached for her hand. "You'd really leave New York?"

Margo's heart beat faster.

Finally, he's let down his guard and said something human.

"Okay. I'll stay in the neighborhood."

She knew she shouldn't get her hopes up, but she so wanted to believe there could be something between them. It wasn't just Edward's looks. He had a way about him. It was as if he could see inside of her.

As dinner progressed, the conversation flowed. Edward was a good listener. Time flew by and a few hours later, Margo saw the time on her watch, ten thirty! "Oh, my. I have to be at work early tomorrow. I better get home before I turn into a pumpkin."

"That will never happen." Edward signaled the waiter for the check. "I'm calling you a cab."

Margo shook her head. "Don't be silly. I noticed an uptown subway stop on the way over here."

Edward signed the credit card slip and followed her out of the restaurant and to the station. "Are you sure you're okay?"

"Absolutely."

She wanted to kiss him but settled on a brush of her hand against his cheek. "Thanks for a lovely evening. I had fun."

"So did I," he said.

Edward walked with her down the steps into the station and watched as Margo slid her MetroCard through the turnstile.

Margo grit her teeth as she swiped her MetroCard. She wanted so badly to kiss him on the lips. How would he have reacted if she'd done it? Would it scare him off? He hadn't made any move toward her. She wondered if he was just being a gentleman or possibly not ready to date again.

"Call me on my cell when you get home."

"Will do."

WHEN MARGO WALKED into her apartment at eleven thirty, there was a note on the kitchen table.

*The real estate man left his number. He needs you to call him tomorrow about the apartment. Couldn't keep my eyes open. Sleep tight.*
*Mom*

Margo was worried. She didn't dare to wake her mother. The woman was struggling to hold onto a marriage that was disintegrating. She needed to talk to someone. Edward knew about real estate.

She texted him.

Finally home safe and sound. Have to call real estate agent about my uncle's condo. Hope its good news.

He replied immediately. I'll be in touch. Good luck

Margo tossed and turned, unable to find a comfortable spot in bed.

In addition to coping with a meddling stepfather, she'd have to settle the condo issue and keep looking for a full-time teaching job. She was in no position to go out on her own without her inheritance.

Anxiety dissipated thoughts of Edward.

# Chapter Ten

Margo returned to the real world when she opened the dry cleaner.

"Hi, Margo," the morning shift worker said. "I left some papers near the register for you."

"Thanks."

Busy wading through tickets to be processed, Margo didn't have time to think about Edward.

On her break, she read his last text message. If I didn't bore you too much, how about dinner and a movie on Sunday? I know it's last minute, but with the London office expansion plans, I'm going in ten directions at once.

Margo texted him back. Mr. Fong told me we're moving back to the old location on Monday. Looks like the insurance company came through for my boss. I'd hoped to have Sunday to myself, but I'm helping him box evening wear. Let me know what time the movie is playing and where to meet you.

She turned off the phone and went back to work. Engrossed in helping customers, Margo forgot to go to the bank to make the end-of-the-week deposits.

"Mr. Fong, please forgive me."

"No worries, Margo. I've been busy as well. Put the Closed sign on the door, tally the receipts, and I'll make the deposit on my way home."

"Thank you so much," Margo said.

With customers streaming in and out all day, neither of them had a chance to go to the bank. Mr. Fong had to leave early to take his daughter to a piano recital.

Margo folded and boxed the last set of shirts, locked the cash register, and switched the sign on the door to Closed. She thought of Edward. She needed to bring more to his table than her expertise at folding and boxing shirts. She wanted to feel his virile hands working her body and the excitement of their first time. However, she was insecure about measuring up to the kind of women he was used to being with.

On the way home, Margo bought all of the ingredients for her mother's favorite quiche. She wanted to surprise her with a nice dinner. However, when she walked into the apartment, Diana was fast asleep.

In a note taped to the refrigerator, she told Margo to fix herself something. She and Jerry had another fight. He'd moved in with his brother. They'd catch up at breakfast.

Margo worried about her mother's loss of appetite. She'd been telling her to go for a checkup, but Diana offered the same refrain, "When I have time, I'll go."

The only quality time she spent with her was on the phone during the day. At night, she was the referee between two angry people.

Margo read Edward's text about the movie. It started at one. He hoped she liked foreign films.

Too tired to fuss for one person, Margo opened a container of yogurt, showered, picked out something to wear for her date, and collapsed on the bed. In her dreams, he was feeding her strawberries while they sipped champagne.

～

MARGO DIDN'T LIKE to work on Sunday, but Mr. Fong had been good to her. Her conscience would bother her if she didn't help him. When she put the key in the front door of the dry cleaner, she noticed the Closed sign was missing. Mr. Fong was an early riser. He'd probably been there for hours packing for the move.

"Margo, can you come back here please?" Mr. Fong called out.

"One second."

Margo emptied an overflowing trash can and pinned new business flyers to a bulletin board hanging on a wall opposite the cash register. She dumped old magazines and made a note to bring new ones.

"Here I am."

Mr. Fong pointed to beadwork on a Chanel gown. "Some of these are loose. Please tell Mrs. Owens so she doesn't think I damaged it in cleaning."

"I'm sure she won't."

Margo returned to the front of the store to find a young man reading flyers on the bulletin board.

He approached the counter.

"Sir, we're closed."

She noticed how his hands were shaking. He sniffed incessantly. In the pit of her stomach, Margo sensed trouble. She reached for the wall phone.

"Put it down and lock up," he said.

"I've already told you, we're closed today."

He lifted a gun from his pocket. "Lock the door and open the register. Do it now."

Margo tried to stop her hands from trembling. All she could think about was staying alive. She walked to the door and pretended to lock it. Beads of perspiration dotted her forehead.

*Dear God, save me from this drug crazed addict.*

"I need my fix. Give me the money in the register, and I won't hurt you."

Margo stared at the barrel on the small gun. She wondered if he knew how to use it, but she wasn't going to take any chances. Her fingers shook. It took three tries to open the cash register. She grabbed some fives, tens, and a few ones.

"This is all there is," she said, placing the bills on the counter.

The robber reached out to shove them into his pocket.

"I need more. I've been watching this place for a week. I saw lots of rich people come in here yesterday. You must have more money."

Maybe this was fate playing the last cruel trick on her. After enduring a fractured childhood and struggling to make something of her life, it was too late for anything good to happen.

"Margo, I need you back here," Mr. Fong called out.

Margo couldn't get her tongue to work. The intruder pointed the gun in her face. "We're going back there."

Margo moved as though her legs were made of lead. "Please don't hurt anyone."

"Shut up."

Mr. Fong met her halfway to the front of the store.

He looked at the scrawny kid holding the gun and raised his hands. "Don't shoot. I have a wife and two daughters at home."

"Who's the old guy?"

"My boss."

Sweat broke out on Mr. Fong's bald head.

Margo eased her way next to him and whispered in his ear. "Stay calm, and we'll get out of this alive."

"Where's cash box? Every business has a cash box," the intruder said. "Tell me, or I'll shoot both of you."

"It's not here, don't need a cash box full of money since most of our business is with credit cards."

The robber pushed Margo out of the way and slammed Mr. Fong's forehead with the end of his gun. "Liar!"

"Oh my God," Margo screamed, watching her boss slump to the floor.

"Where's the rest of the money, bitch? I need my fix."

Margo bent down to check Mr. Fong's pulse.

She pulled a First Aid kit off a shelf and bandaged her boss's bleeding head. "He's badly hurt. He needs a doctor."

# Chapter Eleven

After a workout at the gym, Edward needed a shower. Excited about seeing Margo for something other than business, he couldn't wait until she arrived at the movie theater. He'd surprise her at work.

He dressed with care and took a slow walk to the dry cleaner. He'd dated tons of women and been married for ten years, but as he moved toward the shop, he had the nervous jitters of a teenager on his first date.

Edward knocked on the front door and turned the handle. It opened easily.

He rang the counter bell. "Anybody here?"

The place was too quiet. He rang again, moving closer to the counter.

Margo heard his voice. She walked toward him.

"Hello, Margo. I thought I'd surprise you."

She pointed her head toward the intruder and mouthed the words. "Help me."

Edward saw the gun in the boy's hand. "Son, you don't want to go to jail."

"What's it to you?" His convulsions due to withdrawal seemed to be getting worse. The gun he was holding was literally shaking in his hands

"Put down the weapon. Let's talk."

"I need a fix!" He shouted.

Edward leaned over the counter. "If you've been in a jail cell, you don't want to go back. Give me the gun, or at least put it down before someone is hurt."

The young man's hands began to shake again. "I did my time. No one is going to ever lock me up again."

He slumped to the floor convulsing in pain.

Edward jumped over the counter and grabbed the gun. "Call nine one one. I'll stay here with him."

Margo's fingers trembled as she used the store phone. "Please send an ambulance and the Police to Fong's Dry Cleaner on First Avenue and Fifty Seventh. There are two injured people here."

Edward cut a swath of plastic wrapping off a roll and bound the boy's hands and feet.

He grabbed hold of Margo's trembling hands.

"I'm here. I won't let anyone harm you. How is your boss?"

Margo pointed to the intruder. "He hit him on the head. I bandaged it as best I could."

"Stay here," Edward said. "I'm going to the back to check on Mr. Fong."

A few minutes later, he returned to the front and embraced Margo. "He is lucid, probably a mild concussion, I think he'll be okay."

"Please don't let go," Margo said. "I'm so glad you're here."

He stroked her hair. A peachy scent emanated from the spot where Margo held onto his hand. "I'm not going anywhere."

A few minutes later, police officers came through the front door. The EMS team followed.

Edward pointed to the back of the store. "A man is injured."

He waited with Margo while the medical staff lifted Mr. Fong onto a gurney. The police started to question Margo. Flustered, she had a hard time speaking. Edward told the officers what had happened and handed them his business card.

"Ms. Simmons has been through a lot today. If you need any more information, please call me." He turned to Margo. "How are you?"

Margo's tongue stuck to the roof of her mouth. Edward caught her as she passed out.

Edward signaled to the second EMS crew. "My friend needs your help."

He watched helplessly as the EMS workers placed an oxygen mask over Margo's face and lifted her onto another gurney. Edward followed them to the ambulance.

"Can I come along?"

"Are you a relative, sir?"

Edward hated to lie, but concern for Margo's well-being overruled. "I'm her fiancé."

"Get in."

~

ON THE RIDE to Lenox Hill Hospital, memories of Annabelle's last hospital visit came to mind. After stopping the chemotherapy, her body had begun to shut down. That final night, on the way to the Emergency Room, she'd made Edward promise not to resuscitate her. She died in his arms at five the next morning. She'd begged him to go on with his life. A year later, maybe it was time he did. Maybe helping Margo was the first step.

The two EMS crews hurried into the Emergency Room with Mr. Fong, the intruder, and Margo. By the time Edward caught up, the nurse was filling out paperwork.

"Can I be of help?"

"Please verify the information on this form is correct."

Edward confirmed Margo's Bronx address.

In the space of two hours, he checked the nurse's station four times.

"When can I see Ms. Simmons?"

A nurse pointed to the end of the hall.

By the time Edward reached the emergency room, Margo was sitting up in a bed.

He smoothed her hand. "Should we call your Mother?"

"I did. She was in the middle of an alteration. She's a seamstress. I don't want her running over here. She worries about me too much as it is. Anyway, it's my fault for fainting. I've been skipping meals to save money and not getting enough sleep."

"I'm so glad you weren't injured."

Margo yawned. Her lids began to flutter. "The doctor said I'll be fine. They want to keep me here overnight."

Edward kissed her forehead. "Good idea. I'll come by tomorrow morning to bring you home."

She shook her head. "You don't have to do that. I can take a taxi home."

He brushed a loose strand of hair off her forehead. ."No, please I insist. Let me do this for you."

WHEN HE ARRIVED at the townhouse, Edward couldn't relax. He shuddered each time he thought about what might have happened to Margo had he not taken away that kid's gun. He turned on his computer and reviewed a new client's portfolio of investments, but he couldn't concentrate. His adrenalin still pumped up from the dry cleaner incident.

He changed and did a few miles on his treadmill. Grabbing a yogurt from the refrigerator, he opened the Wall Street Journal and forced his mind to focus on the news. The terrified look on Margo's face marred his concentration. He turned on the television and flipped channels. At one in the morning, sleep overcame him.

A ringing telephone woke Edward at six thirty.

"Hello?"

"Mr. Master, this is the on-duty nurse at Lenox Hill Hospital. You left your number with us last night regarding Ms. Simmons's release. You can bring her home any time after nine o'clock."

"Very good, thank you for the call."

~

ON THE WAY to the hospital, Edward thought about Margo's predicament. The smile he'd put on his face for Margo evaporated as he travelled down the corridor to her room. When he heard the tears coming from one of the rooms, that last night with Annabelle returned. He struggled to shrug off the memories. He had to. From the little he knew about her, Margo hadn't had a charmed life. The girl deserved a break, which he hoped to play a part in giving to her.

He knocked on her door.

"Good morning." He kissed her cheek. "How are you doing?"

"Much better. The nurse told me Mr. Fong is going to be okay. I was so worried he'd have a concussion from the blow that foolish kid inflicted."

Edward moved to caress her hair again but caught himself. *Too soon.*

"I was supposed to go for an interview to be a sub teacher this morning. My friends keep telling me it's a good way to get a foot in the door. Been there, done that, and still no offers. "

"I have a better idea," Edward said, writing a number on the back of his business card. "One of my father's colleagues is a partner in a law firm. His name is Michael Marshak. In our last conversation, he told me his office manager needs an assistant."

"I graduated with honors. I didn't work my guts out to become a clerk."

Edward grasped her fingers. "Margo, since your inheritance is locked into long-term investments, you need a job. It's a good firm and safer than working in the dry cleaner. You could've been seriously injured. At least talk to him."

Margo nodded. "Okay, but it's only temporary."

"I understand."

~

MARGO SIGNED the release papers and followed Edward into a waiting taxi.

"Where to, buddy?"

"West Fordham Road and University Avenue in the Bronx," Margo replied.

Still tired from her ordeal, Margo fell asleep on Edward's shoulder. He longed to embrace her, but this wasn't the time or place.

A short while later, the taxi driver pulled up to Margo's building.

Edward ran a finger across her cheek. "We're here."

He paid the driver and helped her out of the taxi.

"Which one?" he asked, pointing to a row of apartment buildings.

"Across the street," Margo replied.

As he moved to cross the street, Margo hesitated. "I'd invite you in to meet my mother, but my stepfather is antisocial. I don't want to subject you to one of his scenes."

"If you need anything, please call me."

"I will. Right now, I want to give my mother a hug and call your colleague."

Margo waited until the taxi left to go into her building. She hated to lie to Edward, but the thought of him seeing her apartment embarrassed her. He probably lived in a mansion with servants.

Jerry was a slob. He left a trail of dirty underwear and empty beer bottles throughout the place. It wasn't the kind of environment for a man of Edward's caliber to step into.

# Chapter Twelve

**M**argo felt a pull as she turned the key in the door. Diana stood with open arms. "Welcome home."

"Mom, it's so good to be here."

Diana cupped Margo's face in her hands. "You look so pale. Did they give you anything to eat in the hospital? You wouldn't let me come. I would've brought dinner."

Margo loved her mother, but right now, she could do without being reduced to childhood.

"It was too long of a trip for you. The memories of being held at gunpoint took away my appetite. The only compensation is not having Jerry around. How long is he staying away this time?"

Diana raised her hands. "I wish forever. I told the shop that I had to wait for you to come home. I really have to get going. So many alterations to do. Eat, rest, and we'll talk more tonight."

Margo didn't like the way Diana looked. She seemed thinner with each passing day. She hoped her mother would at least talk to a doctor.

Her stomach growled. The hospital food was rather bland. She pulled a few things out of the refrigerator and made herself a sandwich. Then, she remembered Mr. Marshak. Reaching into her, she punched in the number Edward had given her and left a message.

Margo carried her meal over to a small table, took a bite, and called the hospital to see how Mr. Fong was doing. She left word on his cell that she had a job interview and would be in later in the morning. His wife texted her to say she would be in the store to help out until he was well enough to return to work. She told Margo to take the day off.

The phone went off as she finished her sandwich. She hoped it wasn't Edward. The last thing she wanted was sympathy.

"Ms. Simmons?"

"Yes?"

"Mike Marshak here, I received your voice message. Edward Master told me you're a competent worker. Can you come in for an interview tomorrow morning at eight?"

"Sure. I mean, yes, I'll be there."

"Great. Take down our address."

Margo jotted it in her agenda. "I look forward to meeting you."

"Same here."

She opened the bedroom closet and stared at her paltry wardrobe. She'd have to improvise. She took the black skirt from an old suit and borrowed her mother's linen blazer. With black pumps, a white silk blouse, and accessories, she'd look professional.

The rest of the day was spent trying to unwind. Every time she thought about the gun in that guy's hands, she shivered. Pulling a romance novel off the shelf, she imagined the hero was Edward Master and, she, the love interest. At first, she felt guilty indulging in a leisurely pursuit, but as the day wore on, Margo allowed herself to enjoy the read. By nine she was asleep.

The rings from her cell phone disturbed her slumber.

"How are you feeling now?" Edward asked.

"Much better. Your colleague called. I have an interview for tomorrow morning. Mr. Fong's wife told me to take tomorrow off, but I'll go back to the store after I speak with Mr. Marshak."

Margo wished Edward were there now holding her in his arms. He was probably a good hugger too. "Keep your fingers crossed that all goes well."

"It will. You're a smart woman. Walk in with confidence."

~

THE LAST THING Margo needed at six in the morning was a loose button on her jacket. Her mother was so much better at mending things, but the poor woman hadn't been sleeping well at night and refused to make a doctor's appointment. Being stubborn is a family trait.

Margo did her best and hurried out the door, down the block, and into the subway for the trip to the city. She thought of clever things to say on her interview. After reflecting on where she was going, she decided it was better to be a good listener and let her resume do the talking.

While not as impressive as in Edward's firm, the interior of Marshak, Dell, and Conover was pleasing to the eye. Glass encased offices with modern décor and vases of spring flowers filled two sides of a long corridor.

Margo felt a spell of nausea coming on. Aside from substitute teaching and the dry cleaner, her only other job had been working at Macy's during school breaks and on weekends. She knew her way around a computer, but only excelled at PowerPoint. More of a wordsmith, her only foray into technology was the Smartboard she'd used during student teaching.

"Hello," Margo said to the receptionist. "I'm here to see Mr. Marshak."

"Your name, please?"

"Margo Simmons."

"Yes, he's expecting you. I'll let his assistant know you're here."

A woman a few inches shorter than Margo with shoulder-length chestnut brown hair extended her hand. "Mary Ann Connor, I'm the office manager. So nice to meet you. I'll take you right to him."

"Thank you."

Margo followed the conservatively dressed woman down a long hallway and into a corner office. A telescope by a floor–to- ceiling-window caught her eye as a middle-aged man in a Brooks Brothers navy pinstriped suit gave her a firm handshake.

"Mike Marshak. You must be Ms. Simmons."

He pointed to a chair across from his desk. "Please, have a seat. I've reviewed your resume, but tell me a little about yourself."

Margo described every bit of business acumen she possessed.

"I see. Good. Law isn't for the faint of heart, Miss Simmons," Marshak said. "We put in long hours and are subject to the demands of clients, the courts, and the legislative bodies. However, I think you'll find me a fair boss. We've taken on a dozen new clients. Mary Ann is drowning in paperwork. If you don't mind getting in at eight and putting in some overtime, you'll find this an interesting place to work. You'll learn a lot. Who knows? You might decide to become a lawyer."

Margo breathed a sigh of relief. He seemed to like her. The money from this job would give her more financial freedom. However, she hoped her dream of being a teacher wouldn't die once she started to work at the firm.

"Teaching is my goal, sir. As to the position, I'm always willing to roll up my sleeves and pitch in to get things done."

Margo wanted to say it was only temporary but not wanting to press her luck, she silenced her tongue.

Marshak nodded. "I have to dash to a client. Mary Ann will fill you in on the details. See you a week from today."

He moved toward the door and walked back to Margo.

"I saw on your resume that you took several courses in English as a Second Language. I'm hoping you can help me out. My cleaning lady recently came here from the Ukraine. She speaks enough English to get by, but her daughter, Katya, is struggling. Would you mind talking to the kid? Her mother told me she's having a hard time at school. You can consider it teacher-in-training practice. You will, of course, be paid for your time."

This was more than Margo planned on. However, if she said no, she was afraid he wouldn't hire her. She'd do her best, for now.

"Of course."

"Great," Marshak replied. "Mary Ann has Mrs. Markova's number."

"Is everything good in here?" Mary Ann asked, poking her head into the office.

"We're excellent. Ms. Simmons has decided to join us. If you'll excuse me, I have to dash."

Marshak hurried out the door.

Mary Ann extended her hand. "Welcome to the firm. Do you have time to fill out some forms?"

"Yes."

Margo followed Mary Ann back down the hall to a smaller but nicely appointed office. Plants lined the windowsills and photos of Venice, the walls.

She handed Margo a clipped packet of papers. "If you can bring these forms to me before the close of business, I'll push them through Human Resources. In the meantime, let me show you where you'll be sitting and other important details."

Mary Ann offered her a legal pad and pen. "In case you need to take notes."

BY TEN O'CLOCK, Margo was saturated. Her head spun from the list of tasks, but she was determined to meet each challenge.

"Thanks for the orientation, Mary Ann. See you in a few."

Margo stepped into an open elevator, exited onto Park Avenue, and hurried over to the dry cleaner.

"Ms. Margo, I told you not to worry about today," Mrs. Fong said.

"I'm still working here. Give me a few minutes to change clothes, and I'll help you."

Despite the turmoil, Margo had to smile. In the last twenty-four hours, her life had turned around. She had to thank Mr. Master.

# Chapter Thirteen

**M**argo hurried home to tell her mother the good news, but wound up calling Edward. He answered on the first ring.

"Ed Masters"

"It's Margo Simmons. I got the job at your colleague's law firm. Mr. Marshak is a nice man. I think I'm going to enjoy working there."

"Marvelous. I knew you could do it. Good luck and keep me posted."

Margo had hoped for a more personal response. An hour before dinner, the intercom rang. "Flower delivery."

Margo frowned. "Mama, are you expecting anything?"

Diana shook her head. "No."

Margo grabbed her keys. "Be right back. I'll check it out."

When she stepped off the elevator, a man stood in the small lobby holding a red vase overflowing with multicolored roses.

She tipped the delivery guy and pressed in on the elevator button, not trusting herself to walk back up with the flowers.

"How beautiful," Diana Simmons said. "Is there a card?"

Margo pulled it out and read. Congratulations on your new beginning. Edward Master.

"Come, let's have dinner. You can tell me all about your interview and Mr. Master. I'm proud of you."

Margo hurried through the meal. She feigned sleepiness to call Edward again.

"Masters"

"The flowers are gorgeous. Roses are my favorite. You're spoiling me."

"A worthwhile pursuit."

She wanted to crawl through the phone, wrap her arms around his trim chest, and kiss him hard on the lips.

"Keep me posted."

"Okay, the next time we meet, I'll be the girl with a big smile on my face. One more thing."

"Tell me."

"Be prepared for a hug."

"I look forward to it!"

Margo didn't fall asleep until almost midnight. She had to finish filling out the paperwork to take ownership of Uncle Harry's apartment. While she was relieved to have a job, she knew how pressured working in a law firm could be. She hoped she had the stamina for it.

THE NEXT MORNING her cell phone went off at five thirty.

"Miss Simmons? I'm Mrs. Markova, the cleaning lady for Mr. Marshak. He gave me your number. Can you come by this afternoon? My Katya, she is crying a lot. I will clean more apartments to pay you."

The woman sounded desperate. Margo remembered what it was like for her mother. She always worried about having enough money to pay a babysitter.

"What's your address? I'll stop by after work."

"Wonderful. I'm located on West 26th and Tenth. Come to apartment 20F."

Margo sifted through her bookshelf and pulled off a few on elementary ESL teaching. She'd do her best to help this child.

By the end of a busy day in which she barely had time for a bathroom break, Margo grabbed her tote and headed into the subway for the ride to the projects.

~

MARGO PRESSED in on the buzzer for the Markova apartment. The door opened onto a woman who looked much older than early thirties. She wore a frayed t-shirt and worn jeans.

A little girl with pigtails tied in pink ribbons slid between them.

Margo extended her hand. "Hello, you must be Katya."

The girl giggled. With her rosy cheeks and cupid bow smile, she could've been on the cover of a children's magazine.

Mrs. Markova bent low to the child's ear. "You know how to say hello in English."

Margo extended her hand and pointed to a table and chairs. "My name is Margo. Pink is my favorite color. How old are you?"

"Eight," Katya replied.

"She's pretty," the child whispered in her mother's ear.

The two females chattered away in a mix of Russian and English.

It was getting late. Margo rose from her seat to leave. The girl grabbed her waist.

"Please, Miss Margo, no go."

"I'll be back. Make sure you do your homework."

Katya smiled. "I will."

Margo hadn't had a break since President's Day at her aunt's cabin last winter, and half of it was spent shoveling snow.

She took the subway up to Central Park, walked to the boathouse, and planted herself on a bench. Closing her eyes, she pretended she was with Edward on a cruise in the middle of the sea. They were dancing under the stars and making love in the biggest cabin on the ship.

Reality reared its ugly head an hour later when a centipede crawled over her shoes. Shaking it off, she headed for home, ate a light meal, pieced together an outfit for her first day at the law firm, and fell asleep.

An hour later, her cell phone rang.

It was Edward. "All the best for Monday."

"I hope they like me."

"I can't imagine anyone not liking you. You radiate warmth just by being in a room."

Margo now had two reasons to be excited. Her first paycheck as a professional and the hope that something might develop between her and Edward.

# Chapter Fourteen

Any doubts that Margo had about the job disappeared by lunchtime. She was in the swing of things at the firm. She'd memorized every partner's name as well as those of their assistants. Mary Ann was happy to have the help. However, Margo's lower back ached from lifting boxes of file folders, and her toes pinched from high heels. After today she was going to stick to flats. She wasn't used to running up and down the staircase connecting the corporate and preferred client floors. Margo admired the work that went into being a lawyer, but it wasn't her cup of tea as a full-time profession.

By close of business, she'd set up a more user-friendly filing system and noted the temperaments of each attorney. She'd been burned too often at the dry cleaner by customers who used her as a doormat to vent their problems. The people at the firm were different, but to be on the safe side, she'd made a cute sign, All Who Enter Here Please Leave Your Attitudes Outside.

At five thirty, she popped her head into Mary Ann's office. "Is there anything else I can do for you?"

"Gosh, is it that time already? In one day, you've done more than my previous assistant did in a week. Have a good evening."

Margo walked back to her cubicle and gathered her things. Her cell phone went off.

"Matthew Sung here, the real estate agent for your Uncle Harry's building."

Margo smacked her head. "I'm sorry. I was so busy job hunting that I forgot to call you back. I can't move into my uncle's condo until I have a full-time job. I'm only a temp at a law firm."

"I have good news," the agent said. "Your uncle was highly thought of by everyone in the building. Since you're his niece, the condo board has approved you for immediate occupancy. Just stop by the office to drop off the paperwork I emailed you."

Margo knew there had to be a catch somewhere. Nothing ever came easy to her. Even though her uncle's will had provided for maintenance for the first year, there was still the matter of the name change on the lease and a host of other details with fees attached.

"Break it to me gently, Mr. Sung. How much do I owe?"

"Your uncle only required a smile when you move in."

Margo felt lightheaded. Her backside almost made contact with the floor instead of the chair. "I still need a full-time job."

"Afraid I can't help you there," the man said.

"Mr. Steinberg faxed the terms and conditions as stipulated in your uncle's will. You can move in any time after Friday. In fact, if you're free tomorrow, you can do a walk-through to become acquainted with the building and your new apartment."

Margo could feel her heart pumping faster. "Okay, I'll be there tomorrow after work."

"Excellent. I'll leave the keys with the doorman. You sound like an enterprising young lady. I'm confident you'll find a full-time spot soon."

Margo made a fist and stuck it in her mouth to keep from screaming. Only this time it was from joy. She called her mother.

"How wonderful," Diana said.

"I'm not going without you. We can share the space."

"No way. This dream is all for you."

"I'd be lost in that big place by myself."

"We'll talk about it later."

The next call was to Edward. "Hello, Masters here?"

"It's me. What are you doing right now?

"Up to my eyeballs in paperwork, why?"

"The office manager at the firm likes my work, and the real estate guy handling my uncle's condo told me I can move in at the end of the week. Finally, I have things to celebrate. Care to join me? I'd like to treat you, this time."

"What did you have in mind?"

"There's a takeout restaurant in Chinatown with seating for two. It would be more fun to celebrate together."

"Would you mind meeting me at the office? I have a deal to close. Say around five thirty?"

"No problem. I'm putting in extra time to edit a proposal for Mr. Marshak."

Edward seemed to be a good listener. He encouraged her. Two things missing in her life since her father died. She was more determined than ever to fulfill her secret desires to teach and be loved by a special someone.

She was close to the quarter century mark. It was time to settle into a job and a meaningful relationship and leave painful memories of her fractured childhood in the past. The attraction was probably more on her side than Edward's, but she was willing to take a chance for a happier ending than her mother's.

EDWARD HADN'T BEEN SO excited about seeing a woman since he'd been with Annabelle. Margo intrigued him. He wondered if her I-can-take-care-of-myself exterior masked a heart longing to be loved.

He hated being alone and lonely, but he loathed the way his recent fix-ups arranged by his sister Valeria had looked at him with dollar signs in their eyes. He was a meal ticket and entrée into the lifestyles of the privileged class.

So far, Margo didn't seem to be a user. He hoped the passion he saw each time their eyes met would be his soon because he didn't know how much longer he could keep his hands to himself.

MARGO LOOKED OUT THE WINDOW. The summer shower the weatherman had forecasted never arrived. Good. The drenched look didn't become her.

A bit before five she dashed into the ladies room, freshened up, and slipped into a black cotton summer skirt with a high slit and a pink lace blouse emphasizing her breasts.

WHEN MARGO ARRIVED on Edward's floor, there wasn't a soul in sight. She ran down the hall to his office and threw her arms around his neck.

"You're the most wonderful man. I couldn't have accomplished so much these past two weeks without your help."

Her breasts rubbed up against his chest. She felt a response as she leaned in closer. Edward's eyes lingered on her lips. Her cheeks were warm. Her face flushed.

"Ever since I was a kid, I've had a problem with the heat."

The humidity had little to do with Margo's condition. It was entirely Edward. She fanned herself with a magazine and took an even closer look at his office. To the right sat a cart filled with crystal glasses for every kind of spirit from wine to Scotch. Tiny bottles of tonic water were lined up underneath. Unlike her stepfather, who spread his paperwork throughout the apartment, Edward's office was organized to perfection with a place for everything.

She sensed him staring at her outfit.

"You look too delicious for Chinese takeout so I just made reservations at the Regency. Sometimes my favorite singer, Michael Feinstone, performs. He has a golden voice."

Edward pointed to a coat closet. "Almost forgot. I bought you something. Don't move. I'll be right back."

Margo watched as he lifted a Bloomingdales shopping bag and returned to her side.

"I hope you like it."

Margo tore into the elegantly wrapped box.

"What a beautiful gift," she said, staring at a dark brown leather portfolio. "It even has my initials. Really, you shouldn't have." She winked. "I promise to do a good job for your colleague to earn the right to keep it."

Edward frowned. "Several times in our conversations, you've intimated you have to earn things. Why do you feel that way?"

Margo bowed her head. "When I was little, my stepfather used to lecture me about not living above my means. I started working at fourteen. I've always tried to manage on my own. I don't know any other way to earn my keep."

"You don't have to think that way; you have as much right to be on this earth as anyone else. Further, anyone who knows you knows you are a hard worker. "

Edward slipped into his jacket. Margo admired the tailoring and took note of the Brioni label. All her clothes were off the rack. He probably had his suits custom made.

"You weren't put on this earth to suffer."

"Sometimes I wonder if I'll ever pay my career dues."

He held the door open. "You're celebrating, remember?"

EDWARD TOOK the lead as they walked into the restaurant. He knew everyone on the staff. Margo had the feeling he'd frequented all of these places with his late wife. No wonder the guy is so sad. So much splendor and no one to share it.

Margo slid behind a quiet corner table and admired an oversized crystal vase filled with daffodils, African violets, bird of paradise, and gardenias. They seemed to dance in the water.

She looked out onto Park Avenue.

"May I take your drink order?" the waiter asked.

"Champagne, Charles. My friend has been hired to work in a prestigious law firm."

"Splendid," the headwaiter said.

Margo perused the selections. The outrageous prices still bothered her. Then again, if he couldn't afford it, Edward wouldn't have suggested such a grand place. She chose an entrée of filet of sole with polenta and mushrooms.

The waiter poured Dom Pérignon into two glasses.

Edward smiled. "To many more celebrations together."

He waited for the server to leave before continuing with his conversation. "I didn't always want to be in finance. In college I liked the arts. I tried out in the Berkshires. The director said I was stiff. After graduation, I joined the family firm and left my dreams behind."

Margo patted his hand. "Have no regrets. You're a successful investment banker. I'm sure your family is proud of you. I want to make tons of money to do things for Mamma. I know she'd love to travel. I want to give her all my stepfather has left out."

Edward frowned. "Sounds to me like you've given her the most important thing—love."

The pianist started to play a Nat King Cole song.

Edward reached for Margo's hand and squeezed her fingertips. "I like the way you care about people. Nowadays, that's a rare quality. Never lose it."

# Chapter Fifteen

As the pianist continued to play the song, Edward stepped back in time. He was on business for the firm and didn't speak a word of French. He'd gotten off at the wrong Metro stop.

He noticed a young girl sitting on a bench with books in her lap. An early chill of fall air caused her to shiver. She rubbed her shoulders.

"It's a bit nippy today," he said.

"Yes," she replied in French accented English, jotting notes in a textbook.

He pointed to an empty spot on the bench. "May I?"

"Please."

As she wrote, Edward took in her long lashes, which shaded luminous eyes the color of violets.

"Excuse me; I need to get to the financial district for an important meeting. This appears to be the college district."

The young woman continued to write. Edward took in her hourglass figure, long legs, and raven, shoulder-length hair held in place by a black beret.

He pointed to his watch. "I can see you're studying, but I'd be so grateful if you could tell me how to get to my destination."

The young woman rose from her seat. "I will show you."

"Wonderful."

"If you will follow me, I'll take you to the correct Metro stop. It's not far."

After a short walk during which she kept her distance, they arrived at the underground entrance.

"Come," she said. "I will help you to purchase a ticket. Then, I must go to class."

As they approached the turnstile, Edward extended his hand. "By the way, I'm Edward Master."

She didn't offer hers. "Annabelle Foget."

"Nice to meet you. I'd like to treat you to a drink for your help. Do you have a cell phone number?"

She handed him a card with her name and email. Edward's eyes followed her as she took the stairs back to street level. Margo nudged Edward's arm. "Come back to me. You're a million miles away."

He offered a blank stare. "The song reminded me of Paris and my wife. I didn't mean to drift off. Sorry. Wait here. I'll be right back."

Edward walked over to the piano player. "Can you choose another melody?"

The pianist nodded. "I've got tons of them, but it's a lovely tune for you and your lady."

"It reminds me of someone close to me who has died. It was her favorite. Please make another selection."

The pianist did as Edward requested, but the mood was broken. An empty feeling crept inside his heart. Hard as he tried, he couldn't forget Annabelle. Their life together was snuffed out too soon. He didn't know if he was ready for a new beginning.

Dinner was a brief affair with little conversation. He signaled the waiter for a check and pulled out her chair. "It's been a long day. I need to finish some paperwork."

Margo tried not to show her disappointment, but she felt like a cruel fairy godmother had lifted the rug out from under her. All she could do was nod. Outside the restaurant, a Mercedes and driver waited curbside.

Margo needed to break the gloomy mood. "It must be wonderful to travel for your job—Paris, London, Munich."

No response.

On the ride to the Bronx, Margo's throat tightened as she watched Edward dug his nails

into the plush leather seat and stared out the window. She didn't know what more to say so she remained silent for the rest of the trip home.

"WE'RE HERE, SIR," Roger said, pulling up to the curb of her apartment building.

This time he followed her into the lobby.

"You probably have a beautiful home," she said.

"I don't judge people by where they live, Margo."

He gave her a kiss on the cheek. "Take care."

Margo opened the front door to her building and watched Edward return to the confines of the back seat. There were no words about him calling her. She could've died right there on the pavement. Instead, she pressed in on the elevator button.

When the decrepit contraption reached her floor, Margo ran to an open window at the end of a narrow hallway and followed Edward's car until it was out of sight. That song, if only the pianist hadn't played it, she might have had another date with Edward.

"How was your evening, dear?" Diana asked.

"Okay. I'm kind of tired."

She hugged her mother. "I'm so glad we have each other."

Margo took a shower and plopped on her bed, disgusted. She punched the pillow. When it came to men, she was cursed. No matter what she did, she couldn't seem to keep a good one. Maybe she should subscribe to one of those dating services. Then again, they were expensive. She had better uses for her inheritance. If only Edward could see how much she cared for him and wanted him. If only he felt the same about her.

# Chapter Sixteen

Edward couldn't shake the shroud of loneliness that had descended on his shoulders. Everything in the house he'd loved now bothered him because he lacked the completeness of sharing with a partner.

He walked into the study, poured himself a glass of sherry, and pulled a novel off a bookshelf. A half hour later, his eyelids began to droop. Turning off the lights, he climbed the stairs to the master bedroom but settled into the guest room, hoping the liqueur would help him to sleep.

He couldn't find a comfortable spot, tossing and turning and thinking about his life for the last year. Aside from making money, he wasn't doing very much with it. Longevity ran in his family. Memories of Annabelle weren't enough to sustain him for another forty or fifty years. He searched his recent calls for Margo's number. By now, she'd probably written him off.

Margo reached for her cell phone.

"I'm sorry for the way I acted."

"Things happen."

"What are you doing tomorrow?"

"Breathing for the first Saturday in months. We were hoping to go to the family cabin, but Mom has some client fittings. I thought I'd take the bus up there and spend part of the weekend. Why?"

"How about we go together?"

"Fine with me, but it's a bit of a ride. I think your driver would get bored waiting for us while we walked around."

Edward laughed. "No worries. I keep a car in a nearby garage for weekends. Lately, I've barely turned on the ignition."

"Great. I don't want you to come all the way to the Bronx. How about I meet you in midtown?"

Edward reached for his laptop. "Where's the cabin?"

"Poughkeepsie."

"According to Google Maps, it's an easier drive from where you live."

"Okay. How about I meet you in my lobby at eight so we can make the most of the day?"

"See you then."

Margo reset her alarm clock for six thirty.

The next morning she changed clothes three times before settling on jeans and a short-sleeved blouse. She remembered the last time she'd been to the cabin. The place was run-down. Her aunt didn't have the resources or energy to maintain it. If they were going to be there for the day, she better bring something to eat.

By seven thirty, she'd made two tuna sandwiches, a pitcher of iced tea, and along with plates and utensils, filled a wicker basket with a variety of munchies.

When she turned around, Diana was rubbing her eyes.

"Good morning, mama, how did you sleep?"

"Not so well. The pain in my chest won't go away."

"You're a stubborn mule. You take after Uncle Harry. Will you please make an appointment to see the doctor?"

"Yes, I promise. Where are you off to so early in the morning?"

"Edward and I are going to the cabin. Why don't you join us? The mountain air would do you good."

Diana shook her head. "You don't need a chaperone."

Margo hugged her mother. She was losing too much weight. "Promise me you'll eat a nutritious dinner?"

Diana nodded.

"Hurry, Don't keep Mr. Master waiting."

Margo grabbed the lunch basket and headed down to the lobby. She'd give him one more chance. Hopefully, he'd shape up before she shipped out of his life.

EDWARD PULLED up in a late model BMW. Stepping out he walked toward the entrance just as Margo was coming out. Smiling he pointed to the basket.

"What's inside?"

"The cabin kitchen is probably empty. I made us lunch."

Margo felt Edward giving her the once over. With only lip gloss to adorn her face and her hair suspended in a ribbon, she hoped he liked the way she looked. She wondered what happened to replace the cold and dismissive attitude he'd shown her the previous evening.

"How's work going at your firm?"

"I've hired a new head of Mergers and Acquisitions. Then there's the real estate portfolio from a client's Hamptons homes. I'm also looking into opening an office in London. Are you sorry you asked?"

She chuckled.

He caressed her cheek. "I love your laugh. It's a mix of little girl charm and temptress."

"Thanks for the compliment. Your work sounds exciting. By the way, I like the law firm. It's so different from the academic world. The job market for teachers is still sluggish. I've put out tons of feelers, but my gut tells me it will be a while longer before I have my own class."

"Are you targeting any area in particular?"

"At this point, I prefer a private school, but I'll take whatever comes along to get a foot in the door."

Edward nodded. "I can relate. I couldn't wait to graduate and get a foothold into the world of finance."

Margo didn't know whether it was his cologne, musk with a hint of spice, or the way his body filled out casual clothes, but she was even more attracted to him than the last time they'd been together.

"From what you've told me, it sounds like you have a supportive family."

Edward nodded. "Yes, I've been lucky. Someday, I want one of my own, but who'll have a stuffy investment banker pushing thirty-five?"

*I will*, Margo thought.

They entered Rhinebeck.

"Which way do I turn?" Edward asked.

"Go straight ahead for two miles. Then, a sharp right and a winding road later, we're there. Have no fear I'll let you know where to turn."

Midway through the last leg of the trip, Margo leaned back on the headrest and nodded off.

Moments later, Edward pulled into the driveway and caressed her cheek. "Time to wake up sleepyhead, we're here."

The touch of his fingers on her skin made it tingle. Margo wanted more. She didn't want to be a trophy wife, someone to show off at parties and then hands off until the next occasion. She wanted to feel her heart throbbing and her body trembling in anticipation of him making love to her, climaxing in each other's arms until round two.

Margo grimaced at the weeds, rotting leaves, and peeling paint marring the cabin. More mess to clean up. What a shame.

Her aunt's garden was always filled with roses of every color of the rainbow. If her green thumb hadn't turned black, Margo would have replaced them a long time ago.

"I spent many happy summers here. I wish I had the money to fix up this place."

They walked onto the veranda.

"Cozy but rustic," Edward replied.

She struggled with the key to unlock the front door to the cottage. "Please don't expect too much. Darn, it's stuck."

Edward's hand covered her fingers. She could feel her temperature rising.

The lock gave way with his manipulation of the key. Margo wondered if his hands would work her body as skillfully.

Inside, a New England atmosphere welcomed them. Baskets of potpourri filled four corners of the living room, unlit candles graced the windowsills, and a quilt long past its prime covered a worn couch.

"Come in," Margo said, pulling a cord to turn on a ceiling fan.

Edward used more than a little force to pry open shuttered windows. "Fresh air."

"My aunt never got around to putting in central. She's been ailing for the last few months. Mom hasn't heard from her. I guess this may not have been a good idea," Margo said, a frown creasing her forehead.

God only knew what condition the interior was in. Edward probably was used to much better. She was so embarrassed.

"With a few repairs this place could be an attractive getaway. I'd like to take a look around. Can I have a tour?"

"Sure, come on up."

Zipping past the bedroom, Margo stopped in front of a large bathroom. "I have to use the facilities. Can you see if there are utensils for our lunch? I think I left some in the cabinet on the right side of the kitchen."

A few minutes later, Margo walked downstairs to find Edward opening cabinets and drawers. "This place brings back memories of my childhood. My uncle had a big house in Vermont. We used to go apple picking in the summer and skiing in the winter."

Margo peeked into the refrigerator. "I can't picture you doing the former, but I bet you're an adept skier."

"I can hold my own. Do you ski?"

"I learned in my freshman year, but it's an expensive sport. There are so many places I want to see and things to do in life. I've a wish list as long as my arm."

Edward caressed her cheek. She kissed his lips. Eager for what might come next, Margo reached into a cabinet for two wine glasses.

"I'm a terrible hostess. Before we take a tour of the grounds, let's make a toast."

She filled two glasses and gave one to Edward.

"What shall we drink to?"

"Just because."

Edward held out his hand. "Let's go for that walk."

Margo emptied her glass, grabbed him by the shoulders, and kissed him again. He tasted like lemon and spice. "There. Now you've been welcomed."

He kissed her back and followed her to the door.

Tempted to prolong the moment, she shut the front door and led the way down the veranda steps. She sensed this was the kind of guy who liked to take the lead. She'd made the first move. From here on, it was up to him.

"Aren't you going to lock it?"

She laughed. "There's nothing of value inside. Besides, the next cabin is miles down the road. Wait until you see the view from the lake. It's a picture worthy of an Impressionist painter."

She held up a finger and darted back inside.

Seconds later, she grasped a digital camera. "Forgot this. A few feet more and we'll enter paradise."

They continued on for another twenty minutes.

Margo covered Edward's eyes. "Are you ready for a wonderful surprise?"

He nodded. It pleased her to see a smile appear on his serious face.

She removed her hand. "See, didn't I tell you it was beautiful? Every time I come here, I make a new discovery."

Edward looked out at a circular lake framed by a bevy of trees. A dog and cat came up to greet them. Edward lifted the cat into his arms and pet it.

Margo turned on her camera. "Say cheese."

He set it back down. "I wish I had something to feed it."

"They belong to my neighbor down the road. No worries. They're well cared for."

He was even gentle with animals.

He pointed to the camera. "Can I see the picture?"

Margo turned on view mode.

"Nice. You're good."

Edward pointed to a sign that said Nature Trail. "Let's go for it. I haven't taken one of those walks in years. Soon they were surrounded by tall trees.

Edward seemed to really be enjoying himself. "It's so peaceful here. I'd like to capture this atmosphere in a bottle and take it back to the city for times when work stresses me out."

Along the way, Margo snapped more images of nature.

"I've been to the most exciting cities in the world, but I feel more at home here. Must be the company."

Margo winked. "I bet you say that to all the girls."

Edward pointed to a cluster of wild flowers on the edge of another small lake.

He took the camera strap from around her neck, led her to a grassy spot, and explored the settings. "I give up. How can we get this thing to take our picture?"

"Simple."

"Maybe for you."

Edward watched as Margo adjusted the settings and took a selfie.

A few seconds later, he stared at their picture. "You have the magic touch with this camera."

She smiled. "Photography has been a passion since I was a teenager."

He extended his hand. "I think I saw some deer a ways back. Let's retrace our steps."

Margo turned to him. "We didn't eat lunch. Are you getting hungry?"

"Not really, but maybe we should head back. The sky looks threatening."

A few feet from where they'd started, a gray cloud let loose a torrent of water.

"Let's make a run for it."

"Fine by me," Margo said. Edward grabbed hold of her arm. "I don't want you to fall if the road gets slippery."

They arrived back at the cabin, laughing and soaked to the bone.

Margo looked down at the rug in the foyer. "We're making puddles. I'll get some towels."

Edward took Margo in his arms and gave her a slow, deep kiss. As his tongue slid into her mouth, she felt his desire. Edward wasn't a boy out for sex. He was a passionate man who knew how to bring out the woman in her.

"You're so wet," she said, unbuttoning his shirt and pushing it off his shoulders.

Her fingers touched his bare skin. "I should get towels."

Edward gasped at her touch. "Later."

A wave of heat rushed through her intensifying her desire for him. Fireworks went off in her head as she felt the muscles on his taut chest.

He pulled her closer.

The lovers were too consumed by passion to move. They feasted on each other's lips.

Edward stepped out of his sneakers. "Do you have a towel? I don't want you to catch cold.

She pointed to the staircase. "Upstairs."

Margo panted in anticipation of carnal pleasures in the bedroom. He lifted her into his arms and carried her up the staircase.

"Stop there," she said, pointing to a hall closet.

He lowered her in front of it.

She opened the door and stared at the top shelf. "I can't reach."

"Allow me," he said, lifting two oversized bath towels and wrapping one around her shoulders.

A surge of heat coursed through Margo's body. She wanted him but was almost afraid to ask. He sucked on her lower lip. No man had ever touched her this way or made her feel so desired.

Margo was so aroused she forgot about her wet clothes, pressing Edward to her chest. This time her tongue was exploring his mouth. She couldn't stop, moving in deeper.

Edward let the towel slip and lifted her shirt over her head.

As he nibbled on her shoulder, Edward's hands stroked the space between her breasts and slender waist.

Margo didn't mind his calloused fingers. His hand was a rugged touch.

His knuckles teased the corners of her bra.

"Lower."

His fingers moved across the waistband of her jeans. "You're so wet."

You don't know the half of it. Moisture seeped into her thong.

"These should come off before you catch cold."

"Okay."

Comfortable in her semi-disrobed state, Margo wanted more of him. She left a kiss on his muscular chest.

"I don't want you to get a cold either."

Margo's breasts swelled in her hot pink lace bra.

"I bought this hoping one day you'd see me in it," she whispered.

He moved his fingertips along her twin peaks.

She could feel her clitoris expand and contract.

She was about to explode.

The straps of her bra slipped off her shoulders.

"Bedroom?"

"That way."

Margo's heart pounded. Only his touch mattered.

She hoped one of her secret desires would be fulfilled.

When they reached the bedroom, he lowered her onto the bed.

He unzipped his jeans and let them fall to the floor.

God, what a body.

Margo grabbed hold of the bedpost.

Wait, she told herself. Don't rush this moment.

Edward slid her jeans down. Removing her socks, he kissed her toes. The sensation made her wild.

Each piece of clothing he removed freed her from another inhibition.

She was ready.

She saw the need in his eyes.

He dropped his shorts.

Lying on top of her, he moved his lips up her body, leaving tender kisses on her flat abdomen.

"Are you on the pill?"

"Yes."

"Good."

He explored her breasts. "I've wanted to do this since the first day you walked into my office."

Margo guided Edward to the hook on her bra. He deftly undid it. Her nipples grew harder as he circled them with his tongue.

Anticipation turned to desire as he removed her thong. She felt his finger moving into her damp golden triangle. The flurry of vibrations was driving her mad. Margo couldn't wait much longer.

She grabbed hold of his shoulders and pointed to her sacred space. "I want you to touch me here."

"Are you sure?"

"Yes, please," she pleaded, widening her legs.

His tongue moved inside her opening.

A surge of blood rushed through her body. He was going too slowly.

"Faster."

He looked up. "Relax, Margo. There's no rush. We have all night.

She wanted Edward to use longer and deeper strokes. "You're so beautiful," he said, fondling her breasts and rubbing her nipples. "You've made me come alive again."

"Show me," she implored.

She readied her body, envisioning the pleasure of climaxing in Edward's arms. She'd waited so long for this moment. Now that it had arrived, she could hardly contain herself.

Margo could feel his masculinity about to move inside of her.

"Do it," she murmured low.

He went still. "I want to, but I…"

"What's wrong?"

"I…I can't," he said. "Sorry."

Margo was numb.

In seconds, everything she'd desired flew out the window.

She lifted her head to see a confused look on Edward's face as he rolled onto his back. This was supposed to be special. Yet here she was primed to go and lying in a heap of sweat, rejected.

She bit her lip to keep from screaming. "Have I done something wrong?"

He shook his head. "It's not you. It's me. This is the first time I've done this since my wife died." He pulled her closer. "I'm just not ready. Can we hold each other for now?"

Margo wanted to get up and leave but she realized maybe she should be patient. Here was a real man who wanted her but only needed some time to overcome his problem.

She'd dreamed of Edward undressing her, exploring her naked body as she did the same to him. He'd built up her hopes.

She reached for her aunt's robe at the edge of the bed.

He pulled her back into his arms and turned on his side to face her. "I do want you. You have to believe me. I loved touching you. I wanted to satisfy both of us, but something inside of me snapped."

Margo laid her head on his chest. This wasn't the way it was supposed to be. She'd exposed the most vulnerable parts of herself to him. This wasn't the reward she'd expected.

Edward felt her tears wet his chest. "Please give me another chance. Let me hold you."

He caressed her hair and smoothed her trembling hand.

"I guess so," Margo said.

Rain poured down as they fell asleep in each other's arms.

THE NEXT MORNING Margo heard the shower running. Tempted to join Edward, she decided not to after what happened the previous evening. Their love boat was rocky enough. She didn't want it to tip over. She checked the time, it was early.

A few minutes later, Margo saw Edward come toward her fully clothed. He bent down and placed a kiss on her lips.

His eyelids were puffy and his hair was still wet. The wrinkle in his forehead had widened. "Sorry about last night. To make it up to you, I've made breakfast reservations at an inn I remembered in in town."

She walked toward the bathroom.

Edward blocked her. "I know this isn't the way you planned things. I do care for you. I need time. You must understand when someone you love dearly dies tragically sometimes you become emotionally numb. Letting go of the memories can be difficult.

Let's start over by letting me buy you breakfast."

WHILE MARGO SHOWERED, Edward pulled a book off a shelf of eclectic reads. Love Sonnets by Robert Browning. He thought about last night. My God, what have I done? I don't blame her for being angry at me but I didn't mean to screw things up.

A few seconds later, she descended the stairs. "I'm ready."

"Then let's go."

A HALF MILE from the inn, Edward felt the distance between them growing. "Are you okay?"

"Yes. Just disappointed. I really like you. I wanted us to give each other pleasure."

He caressed her cheek. "I know. We will, but you have to give me more time."

Margo looked straight ahead, offering no response.

He pulled into the parking lot.

"Shall we?" he asked, leading her into a large, oval dining room of The Inn on the Square.

"Anything to drink?" the waiter asked.

"Orange juice, please," Margo replied.

When breakfast arrived, Edward tried to make conversation, but Margo focused on her plate.

A few minutes later, she signaled the waiter. "Can you bring a check?"

"What's wrong?" Edward asked.

"I've lost my appetite. We should go back to the city now."

As they exited the inn, a passing breeze smacked her cheeks.

On the return trip to the cabin, Edward broke the silence.

"I can't let go. I've tried so hard, but I can't."

"Maybe you should see a therapist. At some point you will have to let go and live again."

"I've been thinking about it."

He pulled into the driveway. Margo rested her hand on Edward's arm as he was about to step out. "Wait here."

"I can help you with the basket."

"I'm leaving it. Just wait here, please."

Opening the cabin door, she gathered the rest of her things, blotted a tear rolling down her cheek, and locked up.

As they made their way to the city, Edward softened his tone. "I'm sorry, again. It's totally my fault."

Margo reached for the radio knob. "May I?"

"Certainly."

Margo saw the pained look on Edward's face at her selection.

She changed the station.

They fell back into silence.

EDWARD DROPPED off Margo without a goodbye kiss.

She hurried upstairs and called Nancy. "If you repeat a word of what I'm going to tell you, I'll deny it."

"What's wrong?"

"I'm so upset. I met this guy. We went to my aunt's cabin. We're about to have sex, and he changes his mind."

Nancy screamed in excitement, but Margo shushed her. "Will you calm down?"

"Relax, girl. The man's got what my mom called EP."

"What's that?"

"Emotional Problems. Your guy's brain is giving him mixed signals. He's not ready yet. He has to face the fact at some point that she is gone and he should move on."

"My bad luck."

"Get a good night's sleep and give him some space. That's if you're still interested."

"I am, Nancy, but I'm still angry that it didn't happen, even though it's not really his fault. Talk to you later."

MARGO WALKED into the kitchen for a can of soda.

"Hi, back so soon? I thought you'd stay the weekend," Diana asked.

Margo hated to lie to her mother, but some things were better left unsaid. "Edward had to prepare for a meeting on Monday. You know those investment bankers, always working."

Margo looked at her mother's skinny body. The bones stuck out of her shoulders.

"I don't care if you scream at me. You need to see a doctor."

Diana shook her head. "Already done, one of my clients gave me the name of hers. I'm going to see him on Tuesday morning."

Her mother pressed in on her left breast. "I can't take the pain anymore."

"Do you want me to go with you?"

"Don't be silly. I can handle it. Let's focus on now. How about we take in the last rays of sunshine?"

"Sure. What did you have in mind?"

"I know you'll think I'm silly, but we haven't been to the Bronx Zoo since you were a child."

"Sounds like fun."

"Let me dry my hair and slap on some makeup."

While she waited for her mother, Margo checked her calendar. Time to take another pill. As much as she still salivated at the feel of Edward's hands exploring her body, Margo needed his heart as well.

She hoped he'd seek professional help. Otherwise, chances for their relationship were slim.

"I'm ready," Diana said. "Let's go talk to the animals."

BEING with her mother was fun. They had good times together. However, when they stopped for lunch and the conversation reverted to Edward, Margo changed the subject, opening her handbag to pull out a writing pad and two pens.

"Why don't we set up a move schedule? Depending upon what the doctor tells you, I'd like to start bringing my things over to Uncle Harry's apartment. From what I remember visiting him as a child, it was a roomy place."

Diana pointed to a subway stop just outside the gate. "Let's head home. I'll make dinner. Then we can get to that list of yours, although you don't need it. You can take anything you want. Harry's place is yours until you share a love nest with someone special."

Margo hugged Diana. "You always know the right thing to say."

She opened the apartment door to a ringing landline.

"Hello?"

"Ms. Margo, I know its holiday time, but my Katya is having trouble reading her library book," Mrs. Markova said. "Can you talk to her?"

Margo could send out more resumes later. The child needed her.

"I'm on my way."

KATYA'S EYES were red and swollen by the time Margo arrived at the apartment.

"My baby cried all night," Mrs. Markova said.

Margo handed Katya a Russian/American dictionary. "For you."

The girl held the book as though it were made of glass. "Thank you so very much."

"I don't want you to rely on it, but if you take the time to look up words you'll enjoy your reading more. My mother always says you can never be lonely with a good book."

Katya began to yawn.

"Someone is getting sleepy. You don't have to read every word. Pick out those that sound interesting."

Margo handed her a grammar sheet. "I'll call your mother in a few days. In the meantime, go over these rules. They'll help with your writing.

Okay?"

Katya wrapped her arms around Margo's waist. "You so nice to me."

As she moved toward the door to leave, Mrs. Markova handed her a small shopping bag.

"I brought this from Russia for a special occasion. Your help to my daughter is one."

Margo looked inside. "It's beautiful. I love the painted, wooden dolls from your country. One day I hope to go there."

"I have a feeling you will, with someone special." On the street, Margo checked the time. She and her mother both had to go to work the next day. It was already seven, and she had a long trip back to the Bronx.

She punched in the home phone. "Mom, don't wait for me. I know you have to be up earlier than me on Monday. I'll grab something out."

When Margo walked into the apartment, Diana dosed in front of the television.

She bent down and kissed her mother's forehead.

"Hi. How did it go with the little girl you've told me so much about?"

"Speaking English is a challenge."

"You'll help her. I know you'll be a great teacher."

Margo frowned. "If I ever get a job offer."

# Chapter Seventeen

onday seemed to fly by. On Tuesday morning Margo walked into the law firm to find Mary Ann sorting through files.

"Hi, I have tons for you to do."

"No problem," Margo said, hoping she wouldn't eat her words for lunch.

"Let me show you to your work space."

"I thought it was the cubicle I worked in last week."

Margo followed Mary Ann a short distance from her own office.

"You lucked out. One of our senior partners had double knee replacement. He won't be back until January. I made sure your drawers are well stocked."

Margo looked around a big corner office with a view of pedestrians strolling along Madison Avenue. She never dreamed of having such a large space all to herself. It was the kind of room she'd seen in movies. She'd bring in a few things to make it more of her own—if only for a little while.

After a short break, Margo returned to see more notes from Mary Ann.

By day's end, she'd devised better record-keeping and follow- up systems for client needs. Suffocating a yawn, Margo returned to the manager's office.

Halfway there, a cold shiver ran down her spine.

She saw Edward Master talking to one of the senior partners. He hadn't called since the cabin incident.

*It's over— should I forget him?*

Eager to start a new task and anxious to put distance between herself and Edward, Margo hurried into Mary Ann's office. She wrote quickly as the office manager dictated a new list for the next day.

Mary Ann listened as Margo told her of her progress. "You're so good. Are you sure you've never worked in a law firm?" Margo raised her right hand. "Yes."

She lifted a thick box of file folders, placed her notepad on top, and headed back to her office.

A few steps into her walk, Margo felt someone bump into her.

"Sorry, miss," Freddie, the messenger, said.

The folders tumbled to the floor.

She bent down to pick them up.

"Can I help?" Edward asked.

"I've got it." Hurrying back, Margo shut the door and forced herself to focus on her work.

THE THOUGHTS of Edward that Margo banished in the office returned as she walked into the small kitchen of the Simmons's apartment.

Margo pushed food around her plate.

Diana felt her forehead. "Are you okay? You've hardly touched your dinner."

"Yes, it's been a rough week. More important, what did the doctor say?"

Diana shook her head. "The mammography lab is backed up. No results yet."

"Please let me know the minute they come in."

"It's been a rough week at the shop. I think I'll lie down."

"I'll do the dishes."

"Thanks, dear."

As she laid her head on the pillow, Edward invaded her dreams. Margo loved her mother with all her heart, but how wonderful it would be to sit across from a soulmate. Someone who would be there for her in good times and bad. How she'd wanted that person to be Edward.

SIX THIRTY THE NEXT MORNING, Margo jumped when she heard a thump. The last time the tenant's one flight up were showing their kid how to hold a bowling ball, and the child dropped it on the floor. It had sounded like a sonic boom.

Margo hurried into the bathroom.

"Oh my God," she cried.

Diana lay passed out on the floor.

Margo checked her mother's pulse.

Hands trembling, she called nine one one. "Help, my mother fainted. Please tell me what to do until someone gets here."

"May I have your location, miss?"

Margo's nerves went into overdrive as she gave the nine one one operator the information. She remembered what the nurse's instructions from her high school course told her to do. Don't move the person.

She bent down to look under her mother's head. In addition to a bump where she'd fallen, there was vomit on the floor.

"Oh my God, my mother threw up. What do I do now?"

""Make sure her airway is clear and that she is breathing and make her comfortable. Hold on. Help is on the way."

Margo hurried into a hall closet and reached for a blanket to cover Diana.

She caressed her mother's cheek and listened to her breathing. Shallow.

"Please, mama, don't die. You're all I have."

A few minutes later, Margo heard banging on the front door.

She opened up to EMS workers waiting with a gurney.

"Where's the patient?" a stocky man asked.

"In the bathroom follow me."

Margo followed the EMS workers into the elevator and into the waiting ambulance.

During the ride to a local hospital, she breathed a sigh of relief when Diana opened her eyes. Catching a tear before it fell on her mother's forehead, Margo whispered in her ear, "I love you."

Diana's mouth was camouflaged under an oxygen mask. She mouthed the words, "Me too."

Margo took a seat in the crowded emergency room, clicked on her pen, and started to fill out forms. She prayed there wasn't anything wrong with her mom's vital organs. As a kid, she'd watched a friend's mother wither away from cancer. Grandmother Simmons had succumbed to it well before retirement age. The family had enough. It was time for good things to happen.

She returned the forms to the nurse and went to the cafeteria for a cup of coffee.

When she returned to the Emergency Room twenty minutes later, a nurse told Margo she could see her mother. Running down the hall, she walked into a smaller room with only four patients.

Diana was sitting upright and drinking some water. "The attending doctor is a nice young man. He seems knowledgeable. I'm glad I sacrificed our vacations to have medical coverage. He said I might be here a few days. They want to do a complete work up and take a sonogram to see if it is a cist or a tumor."

Margo squeezed her mother's hand. "I thought you had that done already."

The woman's face turned pale. "I got the results from my mammography a while ago. They saw a lump. I didn't want to worry you. I've been so busy at the shop, I forgot about it."

"Mamma, we'll get through this, but you must promise never to lie to me again."

Diana raised her right hand. "I won't."

As Margo blinked back tears, an orderly moved to the back of the bed. "I have to take your mom to Imaging. You can talk more later."

Margo nodded. There would be time for everything later.

# Chapter Eighteen

Margo followed the orderly wheeling Diana back to her room. "What did they say?"

"The surgeon, a Doctor Schoen, wants to do a biopsy tomorrow morning."

Margo turned white.

"Now don't go maudlin on me. It's standard procedure."

Margo forced a smile. "You're going to be fine, Momma."

"Of course I am."

Diana looked at the clock. "Honey, go home. I'm in and out of testing for the rest of the afternoon."

"I'll be back here in time for dinner, which I'll bring to you."

Diana shook her head. "I don't have much of an appetite. Take care of what you need to do."

Demoralized, Margo hugged her mother and with drooping shoulders walked toward the elevator bank. The weight of the world had descended on her. She took the elevator to the lower level where the chapel was located and kneeled before the crucifix. "Lord, we've suffered so much heartache. Haven't you punished us enough? Please spare my mother."

~

OVERCOME BY EXHAUSTION AND WORRY, Margo took the wrong bus. Arriving home much later than expected, she did some laundry, turned on her computer, and tried to escape into her job search.

It didn't work.

She couldn't focus. Her heart and mind were with her mother in the hospital room.

She picked up the phone and punched in the number. "I'd like to speak to Mrs. Diana Simmons in Room 238."

"Hello?"

"Are you okay?"

"Yes, please bring my nightgown, toiletry kit, and a robe."

"How about a book or two?"

"Yes, please, but not until tomorrow. If you get sick, you won't be able to hold onto your job. Rest up."

"Mama, I'll do everything I can to help you through this ordeal."

~

THE NEXT MORNING when Margo walked into the hospital room, Diana awoke from her slumber. "What are you doing here so early?"

"I called Mary Ann. When she heard what happened, she told me to take care of you," Margo replied.

"You just started a new job and you're looking for a teaching opening. You need to save your strength. Stay with me for a bit and go back to work. Doctor Schoen told me I'm scheduled for a biopsy first thing tomorrow morning."

For forty minutes, they read the paper and kept things light.

At nine o'clock, Diana pointed toward the door. "Time for you to skedaddle."

Margo hugged Diana. "I wish I could wave a magic wand and make everything bad go away forever."

"No one can do that."

Margo felt a crying jag about to start. She left for work. Along the way, she stopped into a church, lit a candle, and kneeled on the floor in front of a large crucifix. "Please don't take my mother from me."

Jerry once told Margo that bad things happened to little girls who didn't apologize every time they did something wrong. She went through her childhood years stepping over cracks. She carried a rabbit's foot in her tote bag for good luck. It was time for happiness to enter their lives.

# Chapter Nineteen

Margo wolfed down a yogurt, plowed through work at the office, and was at the hospital a half hour before dinner visiting hours.

"Can I see my mom? I'm Margo Simmons."

"She's finishing her meal. The first one she's enjoyed. Why not head over to the cafeteria for a cup of coffee and come back in twenty minutes," the nurse said.

"Thank you."

After all the testing in school, Margo still hadn't learned the art of patience. She took the elevator to the cafeteria and sipped an espresso. At six, she returned to the nurse's station.

Margo walked down the hall to her mother's room like a condemned prisoner forced to the end of a gangplank. She anticipated the worst.

"Good evening, sunshine."

Margo gave her a big hug. "Have you heard from Dr. Schoen?"

"I made you a promise yesterday. I won't ever shut you out again. The doctor will be here in another hour to go over the results of the biopsy. Even with the anesthesia, it pinched."

Margo squeezed Diana's hand. "Positive thoughts, Mama." They chatted about a weekend away for Diana until the doctor arrived.

DR. SCHOEN EXTENDED his hand to Margo. "I've heard a lot about you."

Diana winked. "She keeps me going."

He pulled out an x-ray of Diana's left breast.

"You have a cancerous lump the size of a peach pit here. It has to come out immediately."

He turned to Margo. "I've already scolded your mom for waiting so long."

Margo nearly swallowed her tongue. "Mama, you have to get rid of it. You can't die."

Margo looked at the frightened expression on Diana's face.

"Are you sure there's no mistake?" Margo asked.

The doctor shook his head. "I'm afraid not."

Diana pointed to her breast. "I don't want to lose my entire breast. Let's do a lumpectomy."

The doctor frowned. "You're taking a chance of not getting all of the cancer cells, but it is your decision."

Margo squeezed her mother's fingers, which were cold as ice. "It's your body, Mama. Whatever you want to do, I'll support you, but are you absolutely certain it's the way you want to go?"

"Yes. I'll take my chances"

"Momma, I'll be with you every step of the way."

"I don't think it's wise with your current job," Diana said.

Margo held her ground. "I'm going to tell Mr. Marshak about the procedure."

"No. I won't let you jeopardize the only income you have until your inheritance kicks in. I don't need you to hold my hand. You'll come after the procedure, and then we'll see where we are."

"Mama, this isn't the time for you to be alone."

"When it comes to my body, Margo, I'm the boss."

Margo knew better than to argue with her mother. Once the woman's mind was made up, all she could do was be supportive. After some small talk, Margo kissed her goodnight and promised to respect her mother's wishes.

BY THE TIME Margo arrived in the apartment, she was so pent up her heart was about to burst. The place was so empty without her mother. She couldn't imagine life without her.

She called Nancy.

"Hi, how's it going?"

"My mom has breast cancer. She's having a lumpectomy. I'm so scared."

"Do you want me to come over?"

"No," Margo replied, slumping into a chair. "Mom wants me to go to work. How will I concentrate?"

"Your mom is a good person. I know she'd feel terrible if she thought she was messing up your life."

Tears rolled down Margo's cheeks. "I don't want to lose her."

"You shouldn't be alone. Can I wait with you at the hospital?"

"Yes, I'd appreciate it, really I would."

"Done deal. Get some rest."

"How do I tell my boss I'll need time to take care of my mom? I haven't been on the job long enough to take a day."

"You'll find the right words to say."

"What if she needs chemo? I don't want her beautiful hair to fall out. This is so unfair."

"Will you stop pushing the panic button; you'll handle the problem if it comes up. Besides you should deal problems when they arise not before."

"Hold on," Margo said. Resting the phone on a coffee table, she crossed her leg, put her hands together, breathed in, and started to chant. I am in control.

"Margo, where are you?" she heard Nancy scream.

"I was doing my yoga chant. I have to shower and get ready for tomorrow."

"Stay calm. Do more of those yoga exercises."

"I'll try, but Nancy, my mom is all I have."

"You have to be strong for her."

That night, each time she closed her eyes, Margo had a nightmare. She jumped out of bed and reached for the phone, wanting to call Edward.

No, she had to work through this on her own.

Unable to sleep, Margo rose at five thirty, did a few more yoga stretches, and headed for Manhattan. As the subway meandered toward the city, she rehearsed what she planned to say to Mr. Marshak about her mother's surgery.

# Chapter Twenty

Midmorning, Margo was so stressed at not being by her mother's side, her mind was in a muddle.

She knocked on Mr. Marshak's door and approached his desk. "Can I speak to you for a minute?"

He looked up from a pile of papers. "That's about all the time I can spare. I have to be in court for most of the day. What's up?"

Margo explained about her mother's surgery.

"Bad break. I lost my mom to colon cancer. Work out a schedule with Mary Ann. Have to run. Good luck."

Margo was relieved the boss didn't give her a hard time. She walked down the hall to Mary Ann's office and told her about the operation. "What are you doing here? You should be with your mom in the hospital."

Margo choked back tears. "My mom insisted I work today. She called late last night to tell me the procedure is tomorrow morning at eight. I want to have dinner with her tonight. "

Mary Ann shook her head. "You only have one mother. I treasure mine. You'll come in on Wednesday. You're a good worker, Margo. I want your mind and body here. You'll be of no use to us or yourself if you don't do right by your mom."

Margo pressed the woman's hand. "Bless you, but I need to respect my mother's wishes."

"No," Mary Ann said. "Bless your mother. I'll light a candle for her on the way home tonight."

Margo put her mind to the tasks on Mary Ann's list for the day.

At quitting time, Edward called. She'd make it brief and sign off.

"I was speaking to Mike Marshak about a tennis match. He mentioned your mom's condition. How is she?"

"Amazingly calm, considering she's having part of her breast removed tomorrow."

"Do you have medical coverage?"

"Yes." Margo couldn't continue the conversation in her present state of mind. "Sorry, but my mind is going in a million directions. I really must sign off."

"At least tell me where she is so I can send flowers."

"Bronx General Hospital. Have to run." Margo locked up confidential files and popped her head into Mary Ann's office. "Thanks, again, for everything."

Mary Ann hugged her. "Courage, dear. Call me when you know something."

"Thanks again."

FINALLY ARRIVING at the hospital Margo pressed the elevator button and headed for her mother's room.

"Hi, honey. Nancy has such a sense of humor. She's quite entertaining." Nancy looked at her meal tray. "Mrs. Simmons, how about I sneak in a pizza?"

Margo rolled her eyes. "Are you for real?"

Nancy grabbed Margo's arm. "We'll be back in a few, Mrs. S."

Once they were clear of the room, Nancy hissed, "I'm trying to lighten things up."

Margo slumped onto a chair in the Visitor's Room. "If we weren't best friends forever, I'd spank you. You know my mom can't eat that stuff before major surgery. I'm so scared she isn't going to make it."

"Don't even say that."

"Edward called me at the office. Every time I speak to him my heart skips a beat. I'm falling in love with him, Nancy, but I can't deal with his issues right now."

Nancy grabbed Margo's shoulders. "If he's as hot to look at as you said, with brains and money to match, I'd rethink things. That combination doesn't come along every day. Guys like that get snapped up fast these days. The only reason you have a shot is because he became a widower at a young age."

Margo lowered her voice. "Maybe so, but he can't get over his dead wife."

"Then put him on the back burner, for now. I'm telling you. This could be something really good for you."

She handed her a Kleenex. "Fix yourself up. You have to be strong for your mom. She needs you now more than ever."

"I know," Margo said, returning to Diana's room. "Nancy, you go home. I'm staying the night."

Nancy puffed out her cheeks. "Then so am I. We're in this together."

THE FOLLOWING MORNING, Dr. Schoen approached them in the Visitor's Room.

Margo was wide awake. She nudged Nancy and held her breath.

"The procedure went well."

"Thank God," Margo said. "Can I see my mom?"

"For a few minutes. She's in the recovery room."

"Go," Nancy said. "I'll wait here."

Margo hurried out the door and down the hall.

"Hi," Diana said in a groggy voice.

Her skin was pale, lips parched, and her hair had lost its luster.

"I don't look so glamorous now."

Margo fought back tears. "Nonsense. You look better without makeup than most women do with it. How are you feeling?"

"A bit stiff."

"Your mom needs to rest," said the attending nurse. "I'll let you know when she's back in her room."

Too drained to reply, Margo nodded and walked back to the Visitor's Waiting room.

"Honey, I'm dead on my feet," Nancy said. "Have to go home and prepare for work. Text me, okay?"

Margo threw her arms around her friend. "You're the best."

"So are you. I mean it. Text me."

A few minutes later, Margo heard a familiar voice. "How is your mom?"

Edward sat next to her.

"She made it through the procedure."

He reached for her hand. "I'm so sorry both of you have to go through this painful ordeal."

It felt good to have him by her side.

"I want to bring Mama home. I hate hospitals."

"I don't blame you. So do I. When the oncologist told me Annabelle was terminal, I walked around like a zombie. I think the worse punishment on earth is to be helpless and alone in the face of adversity."

Tired and stressed out, Margo closed her eyes and leaned her head against the wall.

A nurse approached them. "You can see your mother now."

Margo shot up out of the chair.

Edward grabbed her arm and said, "Before you go, I need to speak to you for a moment."

Margo watched him take a checkbook out of his jacket.

"I'd like to help your mom with expenses. There are many things insurance doesn't cover. Until she can go back to work, you're going to be her support."

He filled out a check and handed it to her.

She read the amount. "Ten thousand dollars!"

Margo placed it back in Edward's hand. "No, thank you. I can take care of myself and my mother."

"Don't cut off your mother's chance for an easier recovery, Margo."

He tried to press it into her hand, but her clenched fist refused to accept.

Edward shoved it into his pocket. "As you wish. If you need anything, you know how to find me."

Margo turned and walked back to her mother's room, mumbling under her breath. "I'm not a charity case."

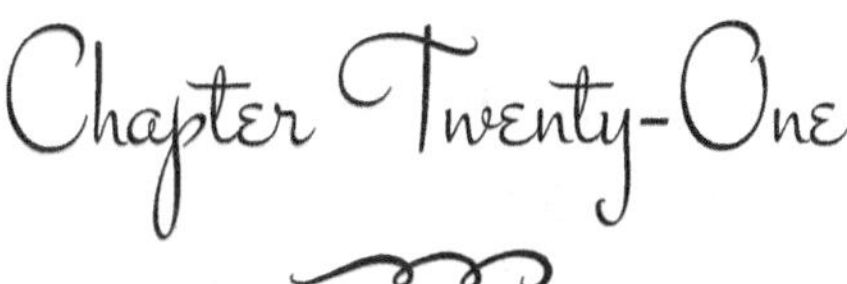

# Chapter Twenty-One

Desperate for some semblance of normalcy, Margo opened the apartment door and turned on her PC to check her emails. Her former college career counselor had left a link to a school on the Lower East Side.

"Yes," she whispered, too scared to be excited. She read the job description. It sounded right up her alley until the last line.

Samuel J. Waking Elementary School seeks a second grade teacher with general education credentials, part-time position.

Ugh!

However, it was a foot in the door. If Margo couldn't soothe the ache in her heart over Edward and worry over her mother, she'd focus on her teaching career.

She emailed the counselor to set up the interview.

The phone rang.

"Hello?"

"It's me," Nancy said. "How is everything?"

"Mom is in better spirits. I'm hoping to go on a job interview, and I blew off Edward big time."

"Didn't you hear anything I said in our last conversation? What did you do?"

Margo explained.

Nancy waited until her friend stopped crying to respond. "I would've cashed the check. Girl, are you insane? You told me you're walking around with ten dollars in your wallet. Pride is going to land you in debt."

"How could I take money from someone who can't make love to me?"

"What's love got to do with it?" Nancy said in a raised voice. "The guy is wealthy. He wouldn't have missed fifty thousand."

"Nancy, my cell phone is ringing. Have to go."

"Is this Ms. Margo Simmons?"

"Yes, who's calling?"

"Adelaide Baker from Samuel Elementary School."

"Oh, yes. Hello."

"Sorry to bother you so late in the evening. Your counselor told me about your background. We really need to get someone settled into the position as soon as possible. Can you come in for an interview?"

"I'll look in my agenda."

Except for follow-ups with Diana's surgeon, Margo's appointment book was open.

"I can see you on Friday afternoon—around four."

"Nothing sooner?"

"I'm afraid not," Margo replied. "A close relative underwent a surgical procedure. I've been back and forth to the hospital."

"Very well, I understand. Friday it is."

"Should I bring my portfolio?"

"Your counselor sent it to me online. Impressive. See you later in the week."

Margo signed off and called her mother's room.

When Diana answered, Margo started right in. "I'm so excited. I have a job interview on Friday. It's only part-time, if I get it but a foot in the door. Don't worry, Mama. I'll be with you every day after work. I've arranged for car service once you're discharged."

"Focus on the interview. I'd wear the same thing you did to the law firm. You looked so professional."

"Rest, Mama. I feel good about this prospect."

"Music to my ears."

Halfway into the bedroom closet, Margo heard her phone ringing.

"Hello?"

"Please don't hang up," Edward said. "I've made mistakes. It's been a long time since I've dated. If you won't see me, at least hear me out."

Margo shifted from one foot to the other. She'd hear what he had to say.

"I'm listening."

"It's hard for me to open up about my personal life, but here goes. My grandfather gave me a choice—learn what the real world is like or you're on your own. I had a lot of respect for him so during summer breaks I helped to build houses for the underprivileged."

Margo walked into the kitchen and opened a bottle of water.

She sat at the table. "Go on."

Edward cleared his throat. "My mom died after I graduated from college. She catered to my father's every need. Annabelle opened me up to love. Her passing left a hole in my heart. You've helped bring me back to life."

"You've been ignoring me. Lots of men have intimacy problems. They do something about it."

"Since my wife died, I haven't been able to handle any relationships except business. Can you give me another chance?"

Margo sighed. "Between my law firm job, teaching interviews, and my tutoring, I barely have time to breathe. The most important priority I have right now is my mom.

"I understand. That's one of the qualities I admire most about you. Your caring nature. How's she doing now?"

"We're both worried about a recurrence of the cancer."

"She's going to make it. Meet me in my building lobby for lunch tomorrow. We'll grab a hot dog along Madison Avenue. We can sit somewhere and talk. "

Margo's eyelids began to droop. She didn't feel like talking anymore. "Okay, but only for a little while. I wasn't in the office today. I have to catch up on my work."

"Great. See you tomorrow. Around twelve thirty? You remember my address?"

"Yes."

As she tossed and turned in bed, Margo was still conflicted about Edward. She decided she'd see him one more time and then break it off. Maybe she should be content to fulfill her desire to educate children and forget about the other one.

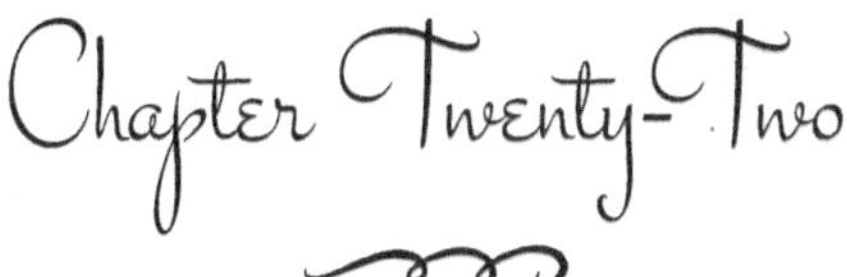

# Chapter Twenty-Two

Margo woke with a tension headache. She'd cancel her lunch date with Edward after talking to Mary Ann.

Right now, she had to call the hospital. "Good morning, how's my mother doing?"

"She's up and walking down the hall," the on-duty nurse said.

"You've been wonderful to her. Thanks so much."

"My pleasure. Been there, done that on my fiftieth birthday. Know what it's like. I think I'd rather hang upside down in a barn with bats."

"Can you remind my mom I'll be there a bit late this afternoon? I have a job interview."

"I'll keep my fingers crossed. Your mom has told me how much you want to teach children. A worthwhile goal."

"I agree. See you later."

Margo headed for the Manhattan-bound subway.

As her train pulled into Grand Central, the conductor blasted an announcement. There would be a delay due to a sick person on the train.

Margo jogged in place as she held onto the pole waiting for the problem to be resolved.

Twenty minutes later, the doors opened, sending a hoard of anxious commuters in all directions.

Margo raced from Lexington over to Madison Avenue.

While pausing for a red light, she heard someone call her name. Her knees went weak as she turned to see Edward catching up to her.

"Good morning. You haven't forgotten our lunch date?"

Darn, she wished she had. She wasn't sure she could handle being let down again. However, Edward was friends with Mr. Marshak. She didn't need problems or gossip. She had to keep the date, or the consequences might blow up in her face.

"No. I'm preoccupied with my mom. Have to run. See you later."

When the light turned green, Margo was gone in a flash, not looking back lest she turn into salt for wanting one more glance at Edward's soulful eyes.

Margo signed in at the reception desk and dashed to her cubicle. The most exquisite bouquet of multicolored roses in a crystal vase sat on her desk.

Mary Ann appeared in the doorway.

"How's your mom?"

Margo crossed her fingers. "Recuperating."

"The flowers are lovely. Thanks. What a kind gesture."

"You're welcome. I've left Post-Its on most of the folders, but with the new filing and client follow-up system you've put in place, you won't have a problem completing the tasks at hand. By the way, Mr. Marshak told me he's pleased with you. It's a pleasure to work with someone who cares about her job. Keep me posted on your mom's progress."

By lunch, Margo was caught up but in no mood to see Edward. Nervous about her interview, she took her mind off him by doing a Google search of the school.

She lost track of time.

When she looked at a wall clock, it was quarter to twelve.

She grabbed her wallet and was about to leave when she remembered she'd forgotten to take home her uncle's old Nikon camera. If things got complicated with Edward, she'd split and shoot pictures in the park.

In the elevator she pressed lobby. During the short trip to her rendezvous with Edward, she thought of conversation starters. Her mind drew a blank.

❧

MARGO ENTERED the lobby of Edward's building

He had his back to her. Once he turned around, all bets were off. She'd never noticed how his eyes crinkled when he smiled.

He grasped her hands.

She pulled back, though she ached to touch him. They walked toward the hot dog stand.

Margo rubbed up against his shoulder. "Sorry."

"Don't be. It's a lovely summer's day. Let's go to the vendor opposite the Plaza Hotel. We can eat on a bench under a tree near the park."

A few minutes later, he pointed to a spot. "Wait here. I'll get the hot dogs."

Edward returned carrying their lunch.

"I have to kiss you," he said sitting next to her on a bench.

She held him back. "Let's just enjoy the atmosphere."

Her body trembled. She didn't know how long she could hold out.

She put distance between them on the bench.

Edward reached out for her again.

"We both have to go back to work," Margo said. *Oh, please don't let me weaken.*

"I'm a bit nervous. I have a job interview tomorrow afternoon. I hope I don't blow my demonstration lesson."

"Demonstration?"

"I have to teach a subject to students in the classroom."

Edward caressed her cheek. "Anyone who cares about children the way you do and whose face lights up when you talk about them is destined to be a great teacher. If that principal doesn't hire you, he or she is a fool."

Margo laughed. "Thanks for the vote of confidence. You may be a majority of one."

She retrieved the hot dog and took a bite.

He wiped mustard off her face.

She trembled at his touch.

*Talk before you react.*

"My friend's mother taught for many years. She said the real teaching begins when you're in your own class. We'll see."

"Makes sense. Just apply the discipline and teaching skills."

Margo sipped the last drops of soda. "I really do have to get back to work. I made a commitment to people at the firm, and I intend to honor it plus I have to see my mom."

Edward walked Margo to her building.

He cupped her face in his hands. "Knock their socks off at that interview tomorrow. Call to let me know how things went."

She walked into the lobby, missing his touch and the smell of his cologne but glad she'd held her ground.

WHEN MARGO WALKED into the hospital room, Diana was sitting up with her hair pulled back, reading a copy of Vogue Magazine.

"Hi. How's work?"

"Fine."

Margo couldn't wipe the smile off her face. "Keep your fingers crossed. My interview at the school is tomorrow afternoon."

Diana squeezed her hand. "I'm proud of you, sweetheart."

Margo made a promise not to keep secrets from her mother. "I saw Edward Master for lunch today."

"How is he?"

"Handsome and charming."

Margo couldn't bring herself to tell her mother the truth about what happened at the cabin.

"You mentioned he's a widower. How long has his wife been gone?"

"A year," Margo replied.

She could feel tears coming. She covered her eyes.

"When you were in the Operating Room, I went into the hospital chapel and said a silent pray that if you survived, I'd give up dating."

Diana opened her arms. "Come here."

Margo rushed inside her mother's embrace. "Oh, Mama, what am I going to do?"

"The only way you're going to find out if this is the real thing or an infatuation is to keep seeing Edward. With your stepfather, I leapt before I looked, but you're more sensible. You've worked too hard to give up your career goals, but I don't want to see you spend your life alone only giving your love to other people's children. You look exhausted. Go home and get a good night's sleep. We'll talk more after the interview."

Margo held onto her mother. "I love you so much."

"I know. Now it's time to give some of that love to someone special who will be there for you in good times and bad."

Margo had to be strong for her mother's sake. "Momma, I hate to see you in pain. I almost wish I hadn't been born—thirty-two hours in labor and now you're in this mess."

Diana grimaced. "Giving birth to you was the best day of my life."

"I wish it were me. I'm younger. I can handle it better." Diana shook her head.

"Don't ever say that. You have your whole life ahead of you. You must be resilient, like the tree in the wind. You must bend when a storm comes so you won't be knocked down. However, where men are concerned, try not to bend too much. Above all, don't make deals with God. He won't love you any more for it."

Margo wanted to believe Edward was capable of making love to her. She wanted to believe that she was worthy of being loved. Hurt attacked the lining of her heart. She couldn't bare her soul to her mom now.

Diana had more than enough to contend with. Margo was still bruised over Jerry not showing up to support his wife. He still hadn't answered the message she'd left on his cell phone. Jerry's favorite expression when she was growing up was Life sucks and then you die.

Margo was beginning to wonder. "See you tomorrow afternoon, Mama. Get a good night's sleep."

Kissing her mother's forehead, she headed home to the Bronx.

THE PHONE RANG AS SOON as Margo entered her apartment.

"I've missed not hearing the sound of your voice," Edward said.

Margo clamped up her emotions. "I'm bringing my mom home soon. I have to run. I've a million things to do."

"Call me if you need anything."

*I do. I need you here with me, body and soul.*

THE NEXT MORNING the doctor called to tell Margo her mother's breast was healing nicely, and she'd be discharged on Saturday. She wouldn't have to endure chemotherapy, but there would be medication.

"Wonderful. Thanks so much for everything."

Margo was relieved about her mother's condition, but her anxiety grew over her impending teaching interview.

# Chapter Twenty-Three

Margo waited several minutes before someone appeared at the reception desk.

"Who are you here for?"

"I have an appointment with Principal Johnson for a demonstration lesson."

"Sit over there. I'll tell her you're here."

Margo's comfort level dropped a few notches. To bolster her confidence, she took a seat in a hard-backed chair and reviewed her lesson.

Twenty minutes later, she walked into the office and beckoned the secretary. "Excuse me, please."

She pointed to a wall clock. "I've been waiting for some time now to see Principal Johnson. My demo lesson was supposed to be at four thirty. It's now five fifteen. Can you please let her know I'm here?"

Margo felt acid churning in her stomach. It happened whenever she was anxious.

Another twenty minutes passed.

Margo returned to the office. "If this isn't a good day, I can come back at a more convenient time."

The principal appeared. A big woman, her frame filled the doorway. Her fire engine red hair stood in spikes on top of her head.

She approached the desk and extended her hand. "So sorry for the delay. Please do come into my office."

Margo sat in a wobbly swivel chair, trying not to lose her balance. She nodded at several framed photos. "You have a lovely family."

"They don't belong to me. I've never been married. "

*Well, so much for small talk.*

Margo's nerves frayed as the principal studied her resume.

A few minutes later, she lifted her head. "So you graduated a year ago?"

"Yes."

"I see you did your student teaching in Harlem. Why come all the way down here?"

"I related to your mission statement."

"Uh huh. Do you have any questions for me?"

Margo looked at her notes. "How many students are there in the class? Any individual issues that I should be aware of?

The principal offered brief answers and rose from her chair. "I'll arrange your demonstration for Friday morning at nine sharp. It dovetails with one of the students' specials. My assistant will email you the subject matter tonight so you can prepare. "

"Fine."

Let's see if she walks the talk.

LATER IN THE EVENING, Margo was relieved to see the lesson plan topic in her emails. At ten to midnight, she completed an hour's worth of content plus a homework assignment.

The next morning, she told Mary Ann she'd be in a bit late on Friday.

"Do what you need to do."

Margo put in a few extra hours to compensate for the interview. Expecting to toss and turn that evening, she slept well.

Friday morning, she took deep yoga breaths in the teacher's lounge and followed the principal into the classroom to give her lesson.

Looking at the students, she blessed her mother for insisting she keep up with her Spanish.

"Good afternoon, niños, children. Today, we will learn about exciting places to see in New York City. I'd like to know your names."

Once they'd replied, Margo felt her neck muscles relax. Mission one accomplished. She could do this.

At the end of the lesson, as she walked toward Principal Johnson, one of the girls pulled on her coat sleeve.

"Can you be our regular teacher?"

"I don't know, sweetheart, but you've been a great student."

The girl smiled.

The principal dismissed the students and asked Margo to come back to her office. Expecting the worst, as she always did, Margo waited in a state of anticipated dread.

"We hired someone in March who I thought would be a perfect fit. The only thing she did well was polish her nails. A substitute is now in that class. We were going to hire her, but she wants to retire. We'd love you to join our family in the fall."

Margo shot up from the chair. "Really?"

The principal pointed to the calendar. "You'll have the summer to get up to speed on the core curriculum. Our new teacher orientation is usually the end of August. Have you ever made lesson plans?"

"Yes."

"Good. Once the fall semester begins, I'll need a copy each week. If you'll call Henrietta in payroll Monday morning after nine, she'll get you started on the necessary paperwork. She can give you the details for obtaining your identification badge as well."

The woman stood to her full height and extended her hand. "Welcome."

Margo shook the principal's hand so hard the woman could see the veins under her skin.

"Thank you. You won't be sorry."

Margo hopped on an uptown subway and went to the law firm.

~

Mentally exhausted from trying to do her job while thinking of all the tasks at hand for the fall teaching spot, she finished another hectic day's worth of work and headed for the Bronx.

She turned the key and entered a lonely apartment. No one to share her good news. She wanted Edward's arms around her. However, been there, done that and was disappointed. She had two choices—sit here and feel sorry for herself or call her mom about the job and be grateful. A few seconds into her ruminations, the phone rang again.

"I'm buried under a pile of paper. Thought I'd come up for air. How did the interview go?" Edward asked.

"I still can't believe it I got the job."

"I'm so happy for you, Margo," he said. "I'm being signaled to a meeting. The children will love you. You have a lot to give."

If you only knew how much, Margo sighed.

She wanted to invite him over for a glass of the champagne she'd been saving in the refrigerator for a special occasion. However, her mother came first. She signed off and contacted the hospital.

"Bronx General, how may I direct your call?"

"I'd like to speak to Diana Simmons."

"One moment please."

"Hi, honey. How did the interview go?"

"I got the job. My orientation is in August. I'm so relieved, Mom.

"I know you want to contribute, but do take care of your health. As it is, you're running around too much."

Margo looked at the time. "Ma, I have to go. I want to do some tidying up."

She also had to complete her lesson plans. It would take a while to make enough for two semesters.

"Go rest. We'll have all the time in the world to talk."

Margo stored the vacuum cleaner and hopped into the shower. The phone rang as she was drying off.

"Hello?"

"Ms. Simmons, my Katya is crying again. She said the kids in the neighborhood made fun of her accent. I worked extra hours to pay you. Can you stop by on Sunday to see her? Wait, my Katya wants to speak to you."

"Ms. Margo, I don't want the kids to make fun of me. Please, come over."

Margo checked her agenda. "I tell you what, my little one. Did you study the notes I gave you? I promise to stop by after work on Monday. Be a good girl."

"God bless you, Ms. Simmons."

Margo pulled on a T-shirt and collapsed on the bed. She loved her mom, but it would be so nice when she moved into her new apartment.

# Chapter Twenty-Four

On Saturday morning, Margo ran out to the florist and prepared her mother's favorite dish. Putting the finishing touches on dinner, she put it all into two casserole dishes and into the refrigerator. She sped out the door to the hospital. Signing in at the nurse's station, she asked for discharge instructions and walked down to Diana's room.

"Oh my," she said, her eyes glued to three baskets filled with a variety of fruits, cheeses, and cookies plus an oversized pot filled with multicolored orchids.

"Isn't it something?" Diana said, handing her the card. "They're from Mr. Master. What a gentleman."

Before Margo could respond, the doctor entered. "Wow, who's the admirer?"

"That would be me," Edward said, walking through the door and extending his hand to Diana. "Edward Master, how are you feeling?"

"Like royalty with all these gifts. So generous of you."

Edward's eyes misted over. "I know what it's like to have a loved one in the hospital. Being in your own home will lift your spirits."

Diana's cheeks flushed. "It's been a long time since I've received so much attention. You're spoiling me."

Edward extended his hand to the doctor. "Edward Master."

"We need to let Mrs. Simmons prepare for her discharge," the doctor said.

"Right," Edward replied.

The nurse returned to help Diana into her street clothes.

Margo motioned to Edward to follow her. They found a quiet corner in the Visitor's Room.

"What you did for my mom was generous."

Edward's hand brushed against Margo's cheek. "Between the holdup in the dry cleaner and your mother's surgery, life has been hard on you. How about we go out on a casual date?"

"Casual?"

"Yes, nothing elaborate, no commitments or expectations just two people enjoying a nice time. What do you say?"

"Okay," she replied.

Margo hoped she could keep her attitude toward Edward casual.

Edward noted it in his I-Phone calendar. "A week from Saturday I was supposed to take a client to dinner and a concert at the Philharmonic. I can meet him for a quick drink instead. How about we grab a light bite and go together?"

"Perfect, if I make it through the week."

He kissed her waiting lips. "You will. I have to go to London for a few days. I'll be in touch."

Edward pressed his finger to her lips. "To be continued."

Margo wondered if things would be different next time.

When she returned to her mother's room, Diana was dressed and holding her overnight bag.

"Let's go."

∽

BACK IN THE APARTMENT, Margo picked up the house phone on the first ring.

"I'm waiting for my flight to London but wanted to make sure the flowers arrived."

"Hold on, Edward," Margo said, handing Diana the phone.

"Yes, thank you, Mr. Master. I didn't expect flowers at home too."

"Enjoy. My flight is being called. Have to run."

Several hours later, Margo's phone went off.

"Did I wake you?" Edward asked.

"Where are you?"

"In the air. I was going through my meeting folder and found the program for our Philharmonic date. They're playing Stravinsky and Rachmaninoff."

Margo rubbed her eyes. "Two of my favorites. I was weaned on classical music from the age of seven."

"Good. I want you to enjoy the concert."

Margo yawned. "We'll talk more when you come home."

"Sweet dreams. See you soon."

"Yes, it will be nice to hear about what's happening in London. I've always wanted to go there, especially for the theater and historic sites. I love little Katya, the girl I'm tutoring, but kids are kids, and the law firm is a very pressurized atmosphere. I need a break."

Margo did want to see the world and be with Edward, but she also wanted to be a part of his life and not just for sex.

# Chapter Twenty-Five

The next morning, Diana was waiting for Margo in the kitchen. "Your role in life isn't to be my caretaker. I'm a big girl. If you weren't here, I'd have to manage."

"I enjoy pampering you."

Diana poured cereal into two bowls. "Are you going to see Edward Master again? I'm not prying. I want you to be happy."

"Edward asked me to go to a concert with him."

"Wonderful."

Margo took a few mouthfuls of the Cheerios, kissed Diana's cheek, and walked out heading for the subway, rehearsing in her mind what she would say to Mary Ann about the teaching job.

"Good morning, Margo. How's your mom?" Mary Ann asked as soon as Margo signed in.

"Recuperating. Mary Ann, I need to talk to you. I really like working here, but when I interviewed with Mr. Marshak, I did mention I was looking for a full-time teaching job."

Mary Ann nodded. "Yes, I remember."

"I found one. It's in lower Manhattan."

"Does that mean you're leaving us?"

"I can come in after school. "

"You're the best assistant I've ever had. I'll talk to Mr.Marshak. In the meantime, I've left this week's priorities on your desk."

She felt bad about the whole situation, she found a good position in a firm where they appreciated her efforts but soon she would have to leave. Margo walked away with a heavy heart.

AN HOUR BEFORE LUNCHTIME, Mary Ann called Margo into her office.

She seemed more relaxed. "I told the boss about your situation. We both value your work so no problem. You tell me what days you can come in once you know your schedule at the school, and we'll set up a schedule."

Margo exhaled a sigh of relief and hugged the office manager. "Thanks for understanding."

As much as she wanted Edward, Margo also needed stability in her life and to start building up business relationships. One day they might come in handy.

She returned to a stack of folders on her desk and immersed herself in her work until the end of the day. Tired, she was tempted to cancel her tutoring with Katya. Then she thought about how uncomfortable the child was in a new school with limited English.

She headed to the Markova apartment.

WHEN THE DOOR OPENED, she was surprised to see a heavyset woman whom Margo guessed to be in her sixties.

"Where's Mrs. Markova?"

"Poor dear, in the hospital," the woman said in a heavily accented Spanish voice.

She beckoned Margo to come closer. "It's a wonder she's alive the way she's been pushing herself, working three jobs to put food on the table. She knocked on my door at one o'clock this morning. Said she coughed up blood and would I mind watching Katya. I came right over.

"Margo thought of Diana. "What hospital is she in? I'll go there now. How horrible for Katya. The poor kid has had more than her share of trouble in life."

The woman shook her head. "Mrs. Markova called a half hour ago to tell me that she was on her way home. Please don't say anything. I was only supposed to tell you that she had to run an errand. She's very private."

The woman extended her hand. "I'm Mrs. Lopez. I live down the hall. I have a grandson, but Katya is like a granddaughter to me. I worry about the child. She talks about you all the time."

Margo felt someone pulling on her jacket. She smiled down at Katya. "Hello, my little friend."

"Is Mommy going to die too?"

"Don't be silly. Why would you say that?"

"Everyone in our family is dead. My Poppa, my grandparents, and my little brother are all gone.

She grabbed hold of Margo's waist. "Don't leave me alone."

Margo bent down on her knees to connect with the child. "Your mother loves you very much. She works hard so you can have nice clothes and a pretty room."

Katya nodded.

"Sweetheart, go into the dining room with Ms. Margo and have your lesson," Mrs. Lopez said. "I'll sit here and work on my knitting."

"Okay."

Katya led Margo over to the table and opened her notebook. "Kids in class don't make fun of my accent so much now. Momma said to say thank you. She's been working late a lot. Sometimes she only comes into my room to kiss me goodnight or wake me for school."

Margo wrote down a new list of words. "Let's learn. It will make you feel better."

Margo heard the key turning in the door and Mrs. Markova's voice in the hallway. She was thanking Mrs. Lopez.

"No problem," said the neighbor. "The tutor is here. Call me later."

Mrs. Markova walked over to Katya and kissed her cheek.

"Momma, are you okay?"

Katya clung to her mother's arms. The woman nodded her head and held up a bottle of medicine. "See? Now your momma will be good as new."

She turned to Margo and reached into her pocket. "I thank you so much for tutoring my Katya."

"I have great news for you. I'm so excited. I found a teaching job. This lesson is my treat."

Mrs. Markova pressed bills into Margo's hand. "I'm not a charity case. Please take the money."

Margo took half and gave the rest to Katya. "Put this away for something special, okay?"

"Oh yes. My birthday is in December."

"What a nice time of year to celebrate, so close to the holidays. We'll do something together."

Mrs. Markova walked Margo to the door. "God will bless you."

"He already has, with a wonderful mother and a beautiful little girl to tutor. Please take good care of yourself."

"Yes, I do."

Margo left, worrying about what the future held for mother and child.

BETWEEN WORK and caring for her mother, the week flew by.

On Friday morning before she left for work, Margo made her mother promise once more to call her the minute she heard anything from Dr. Morell.

At ten thirty, her cell phone rang.

"Break out the champagne," Diana screamed into the receiver. "Dr. Morrell confirmed he got all of the cancer."

Margo carried her Mom's great news into the manager's office. "I'm so happy. My mom is cancer free, for now."

Mary Ann ran over and embraced her. "Super wonderful. You must be so relieved."

"Yes, I am."

Now, Margo's biggest challenges were winning over twenty five third graders with motivating lesson plans and not letting thoughts of Edward distract her.

When she walked in the door that evening, Diana was standing in the foyer holding up a sign.

MOMMA DID IT. NOW IT'S MARGO'S TURN.

"We've put our lives on hold for long enough. Time for both of us to rejoin the human race. I'm going back to work and filing for divorce from Jerry."

Diana held up a bank deposit receipt. "In fact, I put in something for myself for a weekend away. The first chance I get, I'm taking off for Atlantic City. No gambling, just the shows and the beach."

Margo didn't like everything she was hearing.

"Mama, good move with Jerry, but how about if I fill in for you at the shop on the weekends? I'm pretty good with a needle and thread. I don't want you to push yourself too hard too soon."

"I'll go stir crazy if I stay home much longer."

"Okay, but if you need anything, please tell me."

*Maybe it's time for me to lighten up too.* Margo needed to get ready for her date with Edward.

"I don't know what I'm going to wear to the Philharmonic. People dress up for evening performances."

"Let's go into the bedroom and put together an outfit," Diana said.

Margo opened her closet. She'd have to improvise. Taking out a pair of long black silk pants, she selected a black-and-white striped halter top and a rainbow-colored sheer blouse. To complete her outfit, she grabbed a red silk scarf long enough to use as a belt. She'd wear her hair up and add earrings and a necklace.

"You're going to dazzle him."

Edward called on Thursday to ask if she could meet him at his office. Something to do with the London trip.

"HI," Margo said, knocking on the side of Edward's door.

She felt his eyes travel from her head to her sandaled feet.

"You're ravishing."

"I wanted to look sophisticated, but I don't think I'm there yet."

Edward placed her slender fingers inside his strong hand. "All you have to do is walk into the room to excite me."

Intoxicated by his aura, she lost her balance, landing on the couch.

"You're so beautiful and sexy."

*They'd moved fast the last time they'd gotten intimate, and disaster followed. Best to take it slow.*

ON THE STREET, Edward signaled for a taxi. "Il Violetto at Columbus Avenue and 67th Street, please."

A short ride later, he led Margo into a large room with a Mediterranean theme. Paintings with scenes from Venice lined the walls.

Margo could hear strains of popular Italian tunes.

"Good evening, Mr. Master. I reserved your favorite table," Lorenzo, the headwaiter, said.

Margo looked out the window. "I love the view from anywhere in the Time Warner complex. Edward, you should see the place at Christmas. I always take pictures of the rainbow of lights that line Central Park."

"Can I bring you something from the bar?" the maître d'hôtel asked.

"We're celebrating," Edward said. "Champagne."

"Please don't go to expense for me," Margo insisted.

"What's money for if not to spend on someone who works so hard?"

Before Margo could reply, a tall, distinguished man with grey hair shook Edward's hand. "Mr. Master, how nice to see you again," Vitorio, the maître d' said.

Edward turned to Margo. "Allow me to introduce Margo Simmons. She's going to be the best teacher in New York City."

Vittorio bowed and was on to greeting the next patron.

Margo leaned into Edward. "He seems like a nice man."

Edward smiled. "He's known me for many years." He played with a strand of her hair. "Excited about the new job?"

"I hope the children listen to me."

Edward smiled. "Once they see how much you care about them, that won't be an issue."

The waiter poured the Dom Pérignon.

They clinked glasses. "To your success."

She took a sip. "Delicious. Thank you so much for this special treat."

"How's it going with the little girl you were telling me about?"

"Katya is great. She's from Russia. I worry about her mother. She's been in the hospital

A few minutes into their conversation, the waiter arrived with their main courses.

Margo looked at her plate. "The presentation is exquisite, almost a work of art I hate to ruin it with my fork."

She took a bite. "This is the best veal marsala I've ever had." She cut off a piece and handed her fork to Edward. "Taste."

"It's almost as delicious as you."

"I wish I could travel like you. There are so many places I want to visit."

"Then we must start a vacation fund for you."

The waiter approached as they finished their meal. "Would you care to see a dessert menu?"

Margo patted her stomach. "I don't think I have room for anymore. Besides, the concert starts in under an hour, and we have a bit of a walk."

THEY STROLLED hand in hand toward Lincoln Center.

Margo turned to Edward and kissed his lips. "In case I forget to tell you, I'm having a great time. Lately, I'm only relaxed when I'm around you."

"Same here. I can't remember when I've felt more comfortable with someone. "

Margo watched every move Edward made. He was so smooth with people. He made everyone he encountered, including her, feel special.

He handed the tickets to the usher who guided them to their seats.

As the house lights went down, they looked into each other's eyes.

Margo leaned into Edward's shoulder. "This is heaven."

As the music reached a crescendo, Margo imagined their own journey of love, which she hoped would culminate in a physical rhapsody.

When the concert ended, they walked to a secluded area to the side of the lobby.

Margo lowered her head. Edward lifted her chin and kissed her lips.

"That was nice. As the music played, I thought of how wonderful it would be to ride in one of those horse-drawn carriages in Central Park. I always wanted to go when I was a kid, but Uncle Harry had to travel on business and my mother barely had enough money to put food on the table. I've also dreamed of what it would be like to dance the night away dressed in a long gown at a Viennese Ball. They have them in the city, but it costs a fortune."

He grabbed hold of her slender waist. "It would be fun helping you out of one."

People were filling every space in the lobby as they exited the hall.

Margo smiled. "I wish this night would go on forever."

"So do I. Can you come home with me? I mean can I take you home?"

She laughed. "I'll take the subway."

"No, not at this time of night because it isn't safe. I'll call you a cab."

One pulled up a minute later.

He opened the door. Edward folded up a fifty and handed it to the driver.

"Take her home and keep the change."

Before Margo slid into the back seat, Edward kissed her again. Her toes curled.

"Let's make our own holiday. I'll call you on Monday for this weekend on my boat."

"Sounds great," she said, hopping inside.

Margo kept waving until Edward was a pin dot on the horizon.

BACK IN THE BRONX, Margo traced Edward's kiss on her lips. She hungered for him, but if she was going to get up to speed on the school curriculum and each of her students' profiles, she'd have to hunker down until the orientation. She'd make the weekend with Edward a treat to herself for all her job search efforts.

A few days later, Edward called Margo as she was proofreading a proposal to go to a client.

"I miss you."

"Same here."

The sound of his voice distracted her.

"I never asked. Do you like to swim?"

"Yes, but I don't get to the beach anymore. I work weekdays, and weekends are for lesson plans." She forced her fingers to move her red pen along a proposal.

"You'll like being aboard The Outrigger. She has sleek lines. I haven't used her much but keep her in good shape."

"Where is she moored?"

"In the Hamptons."

Margo dropped her pen.

*The Hamptons. She'd always wanted to go there. Steady. Don't seem too excited. You don't want him to think you've never been anywhere.*

She checked the time. Mary Ann needed the proposal in an hour.

"We'll talk more later. I have to finish a proposal review. "

She heard the rustling of papers at the other end of the line.

"How about we discuss this over dinner tonight? There's a concert in Central Park. They're featuring Brazilian jazz."

"I'd love to, but this is my night to tutor Katya, the little girl I told you about. I'm all she has. I don't want the kids to tease her again because of her accent."

"I'm jealous of anyone who takes you away from me, but I can't argue with that logic. See you Saturday morning, early."

Margo was having trouble focusing on her editing. "Right."

Margo tried to pace herself, but by the end of the day, her head pounded. Reaching into a drawer, she popped a Tylenol in her mouth and chugalugged water to wash it down. If timing was everything in life, then Edward had come along at the right one.

A knock on the door interrupted thoughts of Edward and the Hamptons.

Mary Ann pointed to the proposal. "Done?"

"Yes. I was just going to walk it down to you."

Mr.Marshak ran a tight ship. Mary Ann scooped up the papers and hurried out the door.

Margo knew nothing about boating other than she liked being on the water. She Googled the topic online, downloaded a ton of information, and dropped it into her tote bag. She'd dazzle Edward with her knowledge.

She plowed into a pile of folders that needed notations.

By five, Margo let go of a yawn, locked up, and headed over to the Markova apartment.

Excited about her upcoming adventure, she needed to share.

"Guess where I'm going? On a boat ride with my friend. Have you ever been on one?"

Katya nodded. "Yes, when I was two back in Russia. I love to swim."

"Perhaps one day we'll go for a ride together."

Katya clapped. "That would be so wonderful, Miss Margo."

As the tutoring session wound down, Katya wrapped her arms around Margo's waist. "Do you have to go?"

"Sweetheart, remember I told you about my mom having surgery. I have to get home to help with dinner so she won't be hungry."

"Okay, but don't forget about the boat ride."

Margo kissed her forehead. "I won't."

HALFWAY OUT THE office door on Friday afternoon, Margo's cell phone rang.

"The traffic out to the Hamptons tonight will be horrific. I think it's better if we get an early start tomorrow morning

"No problem, but why don't we keep it simple? I'll sleep over tonight."

"Have I told you how much I like you? How your smile lights up a room?"

Margo laughed. "Remember my motto. Show me, don't tell."

"It's a deal."

She signed off and called Diana. "Would you think me a terrible daughter if I went to Edward's tonight? Otherwise, he'll have to hike up to the Bronx tomorrow morning."

"Tell him to drive with care. He's carrying precious cargo."

"Please take care of yourself, Mom. I love you a lot."

"Me too."

WITH TOTE BAG slung over her shoulder, Margo treated herself to a cab over to Edward's home. She'd heard about Sutton Place but seeing it was much more fun.

She rang the bell of a townhouse nestled in a row of elegant homes. The doorbell knocker reminded her of one she'd seen in a picture of a castle in England. There wasn't a garbage can in sight. He probably used a private service.

The door opened.

Margo stepped into a world of elegance. She admired draped silk curtains and a huge crystal chandelier that hung from the foyer. It was probably imported.

Edward took her in his arms and covered her mouth with kisses.

Margo dropped her tote bag and pulled back. "Does that mean you're glad to see me?"

"Come here," he said, lifting her things into the foyer and closing the door. "Tonight you're mine."

Edward carried her up the staircase and into the guest bedroom.

She didn't care if she ever saw the one he'd shared with Annabelle. The important thing was him feeling comfortable enough with her to do what she'd longed for since their first encounter months ago.

She smiled. "This room has a welcoming feel."

Edward tugged at her denim jacket and lifted her onto the bed.

The sensation of his tongue moving inside her mouth sent bolts of electricity through her body.

She breathed in his cologne and let her hands travel to his firm backside. "Please don't stop. I'm so ready for you."

The lustful look in his eyes confirmed Edward's intentions.

His fingers worked swiftly to unbutton her shirt.

His fingertips outlined her breasts. "You're so beautiful. I want to make you happy."

Her hands moved lower. "You know what I want."

He unzipped her jeans and let his lips leave a trail down to her belly button.

Margo gripped the bedposts. Her clitoris contracted. She couldn't hold on much longer. His touch was driving her crazy.

Edward pulled off her jeans and disrobed. He took a contraceptive out of a nightstand.

"To be on the safe side."

Margo moved to undo her bra.

"Wait, I'd like to do that. Slow down, okay?"

Margo felt his hands unhook it. She wrapped her arms around his bare back and massaged it with her breasts.

Margo watched Edward struggle to apply the condom.

"Let me help you," she said

As she covered his manliness, he fondled her nipples. "You're so perfect."

He leaned back on the bed as Margo straddled him.

"Stop talking. Let's do it now, please."

Her skin vibrated as she felt Edward inside her sacred space.

He looked at her face.

His lust matched her passion.

She'd been shy with Sergio.

With Edward, she'd lost her inhibitions, revealing all of herself to him.

Each thrust came faster.

Margo pressed her hands against his chest. "I never knew it could be this good, especially at the end."

Spent, she closed her eyes, and fell asleep.

A FEW HOURS LATER, Margo heard water running.

This time she didn't hesitate. Walking into a cavernous bathroom, she opened the shower door and stepped inside.

"Hello, sleepy head," Edward said. "Turn around. I'll wash your back."

Even the cool cloth couldn't relieve the heat rising to her face. She turned once more to face him, rinsed off, and put her arms around his neck.

"You're the best lover on the planet. Don't ever stop touching me again. Promise?"

"You can count on it. Hungry?"

"Starved. Feed me."

Margo pulled him closer and let her tongue slide into his mouth.

Edward dropped the soapy cloth and met her passion. Reaching for a bath towel, he draped it around shoulders. "You're so wet."

"What are you going to do about it?"

He lifted her into his arms, opened the shower door, and rested her on the edge of a double sink.

"Ouch," she said.

"Are you okay?"

"I've been packing for the move. Guess I overdid it."

He opened the medicine cabinet. "This should help."

Margo read the label. Massage oil.

They dried themselves off.

Edward wrapped a towel around his waist and carried Margo back into the bedroom, lowering her onto the bed. "Turn on your stomach."

Margo tingled as he applied the oil in circular motions to her back.

"Lower," she said, mesmerized by his touch.

"I aim to please," he said, working his hands down to her buttocks.

"That's nice."

A few minutes later, Margo turned to face him.

As he bent to kiss her lips, she undid the towel around his waist and pulled him closer.

"You sure you're on the pill?" he asked.

"Absolutely," Margo sighed. "I could stay here like this with you forever."

They continued to satisfy each other's needs.

Later she asked, "Still hungry?"

"Starved, let's go down to the kitchen and see what we can put together. I have someone who cooks and cleans so I'm not particularly good at it. We will have to make do with whatever is in the frig."

"Don't fret, I do know my way around a kitchen and should be able to put something palatable together for the two of us."

*Like Anabelle she made him feel alive, yet so different in some ways.*

Night descended as the lovers fell asleep.

THE NEXT MORNING, Margo startled as an alarm clock went off at five thirty.

Edward reached over to turn it off.

She rubbed her breasts against him.

"I could do this all day, but we have a sailing date, remember?"

She jumped up and headed for the shower. "Last one in has to cook breakfast on the boat."

They dried each other off.

Edward laughed. "Breakfast is on me."

Two hours later they were in the Hamptons. Margo had read about the lifestyles of the rich and famous in magazines, but to see row upon row of palatial summer homes up close was incredible.

"It's hard to believe all that property belongs to one person."

Miles down a road with the ocean on one side and marina on the other, Edward parked in front of the main entrance to the yacht club.

He came around the passenger side and held out his hand. "I have to get the keys to unlock the boat, work the motors, and a host of other things before we can take off."

"I can help. I read up on a lot of stuff, remember?"

Edward looked to see if anyone was watching.

He kissed the nape of her neck. "You're full of surprises."

"Wait until you see what I plan to wear later tonight."

Margo couldn't let the beauty of her surroundings go to waste. She picked up her camera and walked over to the dock to admire yachts waiting to be sailed. Checking her light meter, she aimed at the biggest one in the row and popped off a few shots.

"Would you like a tour?"

She looked around to see who was talking.

A tall man about Edward's height and age hopped off the one she'd admired and extended his hand. "Rusty Simons at your service. My grandfather owns this sucker. Someday, it will be mine."

"Actually, I'm here with someone. He's in the office seeing about his boat."

Margo could feel his eyes moving to the cleavage peeking out of her summer blouse. She drew back a few inches and looked toward the office to see if Edward was coming.

"Could I have the shortened version?"

"My pleasure," he said, helping her on board.

Margo had only seen pictures of yachts. To be on one was a thrill. When the mini-tour was over, he pointed to the staterooms below deck.

"Are you sure I can't persuade you to take a closer look?"

"Simons."

Margo jumped at the sound of Edward's raised voice. "What are you doing with my girl?"

"Hey, can't blame a guy for being sociable."

One stern look from Edward and Simons got the message.

"Thanks. She has great lines. I'm sure she gives a smooth sail."

Margo hopped off.

Edward tightened his arm around her waist as they walked toward his car.

He made a fist at Simons.

"Try that again, and your neck will be in a fish hook."

Margo fastened her seatbelt and pinched Edward's bottom. "So you're not immune to the jealousy bug."

"The Outrigger is a little further down. As to Simons, he's on the prowl twenty-four seven. He's long on money and short on manners. Left the last wife after a week to bed down a bikini teen he spotted on the beach."

Margo turned off her camera. "I've never seen you so angry."

"I hope you won't again, but it makes my blood boil the way some guys act around here. They think every woman is available and on the make."

"Chill, Edward. He's a jerk, you read him the riot act, and tonight I'm going to reward you for it."

He winked. "I have to wait that long?"

"Depends," she said, stretching her long legs.

"On?"

"How hard it is to resist temptation on the water."

Edward pulled into the wharf where his boat was docked. While Margo gathered her camera, tote bag, and the cooler containing their meals, Edward got to work readying the boat for their weekend sail.

She went to the kitchen area and stored their food.

Around eleven, Edward poked his head into the kitchen. "Are you ready to meet the sea?"

"Fire up the engine, and I'll give you my answer."

Edward returned to the top deck.

While he warmed up the motor, Margo changed and coated her fair skin with sunblock. Grabbing two bottles of water, she joined him on deck.

She handed one to Edward. "It's too early to eat, but I thought you might be thirsty."

As he sipped, Margo watched him steer the boat out to sea.

"A few instructions before we stop for the swim I promised you last night."

Margo paid attention as Edward pointed out the first aid kit, life jackets, and other necessary safety equipment.

"Okay. Let's see. Port is to the left of the boat, and starboard is to the right. The bow is the front of the boat, and the back is the stern. Anything toward the back is the aft. The keel keeps the boat stable. There's one more important thing. Ah, when you jibe, you change direction."

Edward kept his left hand on the steering wheel and, folding her into his right arm, gave her a kiss she felt all the way to her toes.

"I'm impressed. You did your homework well."

She curtsied. "Thank you. Do I have an A, so far?"

He gave her a devilish smile. "I think A plus would be a better assessment."

Margo turned to see a patch of beach with water as blue as her eyes. "Look."

Edward pulled the boat to the shoreline and lowered the anchor.

Margo clung to him.

"This morning when the guy with the huge yacht made a pass at me, you talked about his bikini teen girlfriend."

She lifted a black lace cover-up over her head and showed off her body in a skimpy black top and thong.

Edward could have any woman he wanted, but she wanted him to want her.

"How do I size up?"

Edward flashed a naughty smile. "Give me a few minutes, and I'll show you."

Margo dove into the ocean.

"Come in, the water is delicious." Edward secured the boat, cast off his T-shirt, and jumped in.

Margo turned around to see where he'd gone.

Firm hands pulled her farther down.

The lovers continued to kiss as they swam to the water's surface.

Margo felt a rush of excitement as Edward's hand deftly removed her bathing suit top and fondled her breasts. Heaven to be so desired.

"I can see where your mind is today."

He held up the skimpy piece of material. "No teen could fill this better than you."

"That's what I needed to hear. I'll race you to the beach."

Margo was first to the beach and through herself on the sand just in time to watch Edward emerge from the surf. Her desire continued to rage as she noted the bulge in Edward's trunks.

He undid the drawstring and lowered himself on top of her.

Margo's breasts pressed into Edward's chest. As his fingers removed her thong, she reveled in her nakedness, enjoying every sensation brought by the passion in his kisses and by his hands roaming her body.

"Oh, Edward," she cried. "It gets better each time between us."

He moved her hand lower. "Feel what you do to me."

THE SUN WAS SETTING. Edward nudged Margo. "We should head back to the dock." Refastening her bikini top and bottom, she swam with him back to the boat.

"We have two choices. The forecast for tonight calls for calm. Are you up for sleeping on the boat, or would you be more comfortable at one of the hotels we passed coming in?"

Margo didn't have to think long. "I've always wanted to take a cruise. This could be the first step."

"I hoped you'd agree. Let's shower, change, and see what's in that cooler of yours for dinner."

Edward pointed to the bathroom. "Ladies first, I think you'll find everything you need."

A few minutes later, she called out. "I'm missing something."

He hurried inside. "What?"

Margo pulled him into the shower. "You."

Discarding his trunks, Edward turned on the water. "I feel like a deprived kid let loose in a candy store."

Margo wet a sponge. "Turn around. I'll do my best to make this sweet."

DINNER WAS MORE THAN SATISFACTORY. However, when Edward offered to drive down the road to an ice cream place for dessert, Margo told him she'd brought something on board.

"I didn't see it in the cooler or refrigerator."

"Trust me. It's better than any candy on earth, but you'll have to give me a few minutes."

While Edward read in the galley, Margo changed in the bedroom.

"I'm ready," she called out.

Edward pushed back a beaded curtain hanging over the doorway and stared at the vision on the bed.

Margo wore a red thong with black stockings held in place by red garters. Her hair was captured in a red ribbon. Black and red heels graced her slender feet. A red ribbon circled her breasts, which were held in place by a big bow.

"Come here, handsome, and enjoy your dessert."

Edward felt a bulge in his pants. "All of this for me?"

He worked his way from her feet; he untied the ribbon and licked the chocolate whipped cream from the tips of her breasts. "What will you do for an encore?"

She laughed and rolled over so he could taste the rest of her magnificent body.

THE NEXT MORNING Margo handed Edward the empty cooler. "I hate to go back to the city. Can't we stay for another day?"

"I'm afraid not. I have to be in London for a meeting on Tuesday."

She waited in the car while Edward returned the keys to the office.

"I hate it but you're right. I still have tons of work to do on my lesson plans. Then, there's the move into the new place. I've been putting it off until Mom was in better shape and Katya felt more confident about her English. How long will you be overseas?"

Edward inserted a jazz CD into the slot as they drove back to the city. "Don't know. The general manager is a go-getter. He wants to open branches in Rome and Tokyo by the second quarter of next year."

"Sounds rather ambitious to me."

He caressed her cheek. "Wherever I am, you'll be on my mind. By the way, can I have another sweet dessert like the one you gave me the next time?"

She pinched his bottom. "It depends on how naughty my mood is."

When the traffic light turned red, he leaned over to kiss her lips. "I hope very naughty."

A COUPLE HOURS later they reached New York City, and despite Margo's objections, Edward insisted on dropping her off in the Bronx.

"I'll call you every day from London," he said, holding her close.

"No, you won't. It would cost a fortune. You'll call when you can, and I'll be here thinking of you, remembering how my skin tingles when you touch me, and planning more surprises."

"A reason not to stay overseas too long."

"Kiss me, Edward."

He tilted her head back and gave her a long kiss that lingered on her lips as she watched his car fade away.

# Chapter Twenty-Six

On Monday morning, Edward called Margo to tell her his trip to London had to be postponed. "Let's pick up where we left off on the boat."

Margo freaked when she saw the hour—eight o'clock. "Yipes, I told Mary Ann I'd be in at seven to finish up a special project for the boss. I'll let you know later on about tonight, okay?"

"Sure," he replied. He sounded disappointed, but priorities first. She had to support herself until the teaching job started.

Margo called the office.

"Hello?" the office manager said.

"It's Margo. I'm running late but I'm on my way now."

"I know you're under a lot of pressure between teaching, coming here, and your mom."

As much as Margo didn't envision a career in law, she'd miss the camaraderie she had with her co-workers.

When Margo walked into the law firm nearly at ten a pile of work occupied the center of her desk, most of it photocopying and filing. She began to appreciate the prospect of her new

teaching job. At least she could use her brain. Then again, she wasn't a lawyer and paralegals had it rough. She told herself to be grateful for the paychecks and keep on going.

At five, Margo was ready to call it a day.

Joe Montalbo, a new recruit, who had been eyeing Margo for a week made his move.

"Hi, baby doll. How about you and I go out for a drink after work tonight?"

Margo pushed his hand off her arm. "How about you get lost?"

"Is that a way to talk to an up and coming future partner?"

She reached for the desk phone and called the security guard who appeared in the doorway with Mary Ann.

"When are you frat boys ever going to learn," Mary Ann said. "Female employees are not here to satisfy your sexual urges. Clean out your desk and get out."

"Screw you. I quit," Joe said as he walked toward the elevator, giving them the finger.

Mary Ann turned to Margo. "Are you okay?"

"Yes, I think so."

"The nerve of that guy. The moment he opened his mouth I didn't think he was right for the firm, but one of the other partners was doing a friend a favor."

"Thanks for the rescue."

"Anytime, honey. How's your mom?"

"Back at work and on her way to feeling a lot better about her appearance."

"Glad to hear it. Take a tip from someone older and wiser. Find a nice guy to snuggle up with so you don't end up married to your work."

Margo had never had an incident at work before. It shook her up more than she realized. She called Edward.

"Hi, what's up?"

"Something happened at work. Can I see you for a few minutes? I'm kind of out of it."

"I'll be waiting."

Remembering what Mary Ann had said, Margo realized how much she needed Edward.

~

BY THE TIME Margo reached Edward's office, she had a nervous stomach. That jerk could've hurt her.

He closed the door and embraced her.

*I get the chills every time I think of what could've happened with that guy.*

"Come, I'm taking you to my house. Have you eaten anything?"

Margo shook her head. "No."

Edward hailed a cab. A few minutes later, they were at the townhouse. He held her tight.

"Don't let go."

"I have to call my mom. I'm all she has. She worries about me." Margo reached into her tote for her cell. "It's me. I'm with Edward."

"Are you okay?"

"Yes. Some fool in the office was out of line. I'll fill you in tomorrow ma, bye."

Margo turned to Edward.

"Do you have a garden?"

"What?"

"When I was here, I saw doors leading to a patio."

Edward pointed. "Yes, it's over there."

"Can I see it?"

"Sure."

Edward walked over to a wrought iron and glass door, turned the handle, and reached for a light switch.

Margo went outside and looked at a huge glass-topped table and chairs on a sizeable concrete deck surrounded by rose bushes. "Lovely."

She noticed a barbecue grill off to the side. "Do you use it?"

"Haven't had a reason to use it for quite a while."

He followed her back into the house. "You sure I can't make you something to eat?"

"A glass of wine."

Edward led her into a sunken living room surrounded by yards of silk drapes suspended from gold hooks.

Margo sank into a leather couch across from a bar stocked with, from what she could see, every kind of wine and liquor.

He held up a bottle. "Will Chablis do?"

"Yes. I need something to calm my nerves."

He poured and handed her a tall glass. "Please stay with me tonight."

"If you wouldn't mind."

"Mind? This is where you belong."

Margo could barely keep her eyes open as they walked upstairs to a cavernous bedroom.

"Wow, this is a huge room."

She pointed to the four-poster bed. "Looks comfortable."

"It was for many years. Not anymore, this is why I sleep in the guest room."

Margo went to the bed, "Come, and hold me."

Edward got on the bed and pulled her into his arms.

Margo looked into the eyes of her lover. "The only time I feel safe and whole is when I'm with you. Don't you know that by now?"

"I'm glad to hear it. I hope you'll make more room for me in your life. I'm seeing a professional to sort out my issues."

Margo fell asleep in Edward's arms. It felt good to have her there.

# Chapter Twenty-Seven

When the alarm clock went off at eight the next morning, Margo stretched her arms in search of Edward. She heard the shower running.

Her cell phone rang.

"Ms. Simmons?"

"Yes. Who is calling?"

"Mrs. Lopez, remember me?"

"Yes, how are you? Is Katya okay?"

"Yes, but I'm at the hospital. Her mother had a heart attack. There's no one to watch Katya while I wait for word on her mom. I need your help."

"Of course. I'll be there in a little while."

Margo knocked on the bathroom door.

Edward emerged fully clothed. "What's wrong? Your face is flushed."

"Katya's mother had a heart attack. The poor kid is with a neighbor in the hospital. I'll call the office to tell them I'll be in a bit late. I hope they don't fire me, but I have to go."

Edward followed her down the stairs and looked out the foyer window. "It's raining hard. You'll get soaked. Let me call Roger to bring the car around."

Margo opened the closet door and grabbed her blazer. "No time."

Edward reached for his cell phone, house keys, and two umbrellas. "Then let's go."

"Trying to keep up with you is like dancing in a sandstorm."

By the time they reached the subway, Edward was winded.

"What hospital?"

"Bronx General."

He kissed her fingertips. "She'll pull through."

Margo rubbed a small crucifix around her neck. "You don't understand. Katya has no one here. The authorities will put her someplace awful. That's what they do. I read about it in the papers all the time."

"Try to stay calm. I know some people I can call who can pressure them to make sure she is properly placed"

All Margo could think of was Katya being led away by Child Protective Services Staffers and placed into the foster care system.

"Here we go again," Edward muttered.

He followed Margo up the stairs and over to a bus stop for the last leg of the trip to Bronx General.


Margo's palms began to sweat as she hurried over to the Admission Desk. Her throat went dry. "I'd like to know how Mrs. Markova is doing."

"Are you a member of the family?"

"Sort of. I tutor her daughter, Katya."

Before the attending nurse could reply, Margo heard a familiar voice. "I knew you'd come," Katya said, grabbing hold of Margo's waist.

She bent down to the child's eye level. "Are you being a good girl and listening to Mrs. Lopez?"

"Katya is helping me with my English," Mrs. Lopez said.

She pulled Margo aside and pointed to Edward. "Who's that?"

"A friend."

"Can he keep the little one occupied while we talk?"

Margo's stomach began to churn. "What's wrong?"

Mrs. Lopez bit down on her lower lip. "The child is smart and picks up on everything. It's best not to talk in front of her."

Margo walked back to the nurse's station where Edward had engaged the girl in conversation.

She gave Edward a meaningful glance and said, "Mr. Master didn't have breakfast. How would you like to keep him company while he has something to eat?"

"Sure, but you promise to get me when Mama wakes up?"

"Of course."

Edward held out his hand. "I want to hear all about your country. Miss Simmons tells me that you come from Minsk. I've never been there."

Katya nodded. "I want to see my mother."

"You will real soon but first let's find the cafeteria."

Margo breathed a sigh of relief as the two headed for the cafeteria. She turned back to Mrs. Lopez. "Tell me the truth."

The neighbor wiped tears from her eyes. "She didn't have a heart attack. She has advanced stomach cancer. Never told anyone. Early this morning, the poor child knocked on my door. She was terrified. I called nine one one. Mrs. Markova doesn't have long to go before she enters the gates of heaven. I only hope she wakes so Katya can say goodbye."

Margo was so worried it was hard for her to speak. "We should go back to Mrs. Markova's room to see if she's woken up."

Mrs. Lopez nodded.

Fifteen minutes into their wait, the patient opened her eyes. She beckoned Margo to come closer.

The poor woman spoke in between breaths of forced air in her nose. "Bring Katya."

Margo raced down two flights of stairs to the cafeteria.

Edward and Katya sat talking as the child sipped a container of chocolate milk.

Margo put her arm around the child. "Katya, your Mommy wants to speak to you."

Hand in hand, they hurried to an elevator with Edward following close behind.

"Is Mommy going to come home soon?"

Words failed Margo.

Back in the room, Mrs. Lopez was on her knees by the side of the woman's bed. She held her rosary beads and prayed.

Seeing Katya, Mrs. Markova lifted her head. "Come here, my darling daughter."

Margo lifted Katya onto the bed and turned to Mrs. Lopez. "I think we should give them some privacy."

"Si," the neighbor said. "If you need us, we'll be in the Waiting Room."

Margo crossed herself. Thank God Mama is going to be okay. I don't know what I'd do if I lost her.

A half hour later, the attending nurse approached Margo. "It's over. Mrs. Markova is gone."

"Oh no," Margo cried. "What will happen to her daughter?"

"I'm sure CPS will assign her to a good foster home.

"I hope you are right," Margo said, lifting her head to see Edward approaching. "Mrs. Markova has passed away."

"I'm sure the authorities will find a good home for Katya."

"I'm sure they won't. I need to speak to someone in the firm about becoming Katya's foster mother. I wish I knew what's in Mrs. Markova will. I have to protect Katya."

Edward cupped Margo's chin in his hands. "You're serious about this?"

"Yes. My real father left me too soon, and, like Mrs. Markova, my mother had to work long hours to support us. The child's been through enough."

"Margo, you can't protect everyone."

"I'm not, I'm only talking about one little girl."

While Mrs. Lopez and Margo helped the nurse to fill out the death certificate, Edward went to get Katya.

She clung to her mother's lifeless body. "Wake up, Mama."

Edward lifted the child into his arms and over to the Waiting

Room. "I'm not going to tell you to stop crying. I cried when my wife died. I missed her a lot. Then, I realized if you love someone, they never leave you."

Katya rubbed red eyes. "You mean Mama is still with me?"

"Yes always, in spirit and in your heart," Edward said, handing her the handkerchief in his jacket pocket. "There's an old Chinese saying that loved ones are never dead as long as someone remembers them. So you keep Mama in your heart and she will always be with you."

"But I'll have to wait until I get to heaven to see her again." Tears flowed from the child's eyes. "It's not fair."

By the time Margo returned, Katya was asleep in Edward's arms.

"Where is Mrs. Lopez?"

"She had to pick up her grandson from school. Katya will stay with her until other arrangements with CPS have been made."

Margo took the child. "Right now, I need to call the office to let Mary Ann know what happened here and take care of Katya until Mrs. Lopez returns. We'll go to my mom's apartment."

"Mom, are you okay?"

"Yes," Diana said. "I can't take all the air conditioning in the store. I felt a cold coming on so I decided to get more rest. "

She looked at Katya. "What is going on?"

Margo whispered in her ear. "Her mother died a little while ago."

Diana turned to Edward. "Can you lay the child down in my bedroom and watch her for a few minutes? We won't keep you long, but I need to speak to Margo."

"Of course."

Margo sat next to her mother. "I'm going to ask Mr. Marshak for details on becoming Katya's guardian."

She saw the worried look on Diana's face. "I know how much you care for this child, but I don't want you to run your health into the ground, or ignore Mr. Master. He appears to be a very thoughtful, caring man. Take it from me. They don't come along every day. You should be at work."

"I know Mama."

Edward beckoned to Margo. "I need to get going. Will you be okay?"

"Yes. I'll be in touch. Thanks for everything."

A quick kiss on the cheek, and he was gone.

# Chapter Twenty-Eight

On her break the next day, Margo called Katya's school and spoke with the principal about Mrs. Markova's passing. They agreed, with the foster parents' permission, to put the child into an extended hour's program once school started so Margo could tutor her after work. The thought of Katya living with strangers made her sick to her stomach.

~

LATER AFTER WORK, she headed to Mrs. Lopez's apartment to explain to Katya that she would be placed in a foster home, but Margo would see her every day after class when school started.

Katya began to cry. "I'll be the only one in the class without a mommy."

Mrs. Lopez pulled her aside. "I called the school today. They're going to arrange for a counselor to speak to Katya."

Margo returned to where the girl was staring at a wedding picture of her mother.

"I know what it's like to lose a parent. My father left when I was only five."

"Did you cry too?"

"Yes. I know no one can ever take the place of a mother, but I'm here for you and so is Mrs. Lopez. Mr. Master likes you too. He wants to take us to the circus when you're feeling better."

"Okay, I guess, but it would be more fun if Mommy was with us."

"How would you like to live with me?"

"I have to ask Mrs. Lopez first."

It wasn't the reaction Margo expected. Aware the child had suffered a great trauma, she'd hoped Katya would've trusted her enough to know how much she wanted her. With downcast eyes, she went to her apartment and left a message for Nancy to call her about help with the move. In all the tumult, she'd almost forgotten about the condo.

Edward came to mind as a potential father. Margo saw caring for Katya in his actions, but in the back of her mind, she had a feeling he wanted an exclusive that didn't include kids.

Chapter Twenty-Nine

B y lunchtime, the weight of the world had descended on Edward's shoulders. There was new discord in the London office. One of the founding partners wanted to divest.

Dr. Cynthia Howard, the therapist he'd researched but couldn't get a hold of, finally called. "Hello, Mr. Master, I have a cancellation this evening at seven."

If he didn't get some rest soon, he wouldn't have the energy to resolve all of the issues in the firm.

"I'll take it. I mean, I'll be there."

It was time to walk the talk. Edward stared at a photograph of Annabelle in her wedding gown. Outlining her face with his finger, he opened the bottom drawer of his desk and laid the frame on top of file folders. Hopefully, the therapist could help.

He checked his messages before going into yet another stressful meeting. There was a text from Margo. *Katya is devastated over losing her mom. I think we should postpone the circus.*

He wanted Margo in his life, but he didn't know if he was ready to bring a child into a new relationship, especially one that wasn't his own.

EDWARD ARRIVED a few minutes early to his appointment. Taking a seat, he flipped through pages of an old copy the New Yorker Magazine. Until Annabelle's death, he'd never had a reason to see a counselor so he didn't know what to expect. A minute to seven the door opened onto a diminutive woman. The therapist extended her hand. "Hello, I'm Dr. Marion Samson. Dr. Howard had an emergency. She briefed me on your situation. I hope you don't mind the last-minute change."

Edward couldn't back out if he wanted to hold onto Margo.

"Nice to meet you," he replied, following her into a room filled with books and plants. Strains of Mozart played in the background.

"I hope you don't mind the music. Many of my patients tell me it helps them to filter out the loudness of the city."

"No," Edward replied. "I love classical music."

Dr. Samson opened a pad and clicked on her pen. "How may I help you, Mr. Master?"

"My wife died a year ago. I withdrew from the world and sat in the dark for about seven months, trying to decide if I wanted to live or die. The minute I met her, quite by accident, ten years ago in Paris, I knew we would be soulmates. Her untimely death of cancer last year at thirty devastated me."

Dr. Samson jotted down notes. "I'm sorry for your loss. Is getting over your wife's death the problem?"

Edward loosened his tie. "Yes, I was ready to give up on life. Then, I met a lovely girl. She came to my office about investing her inheritance. We've become close and I think I'm falling in love with her."

"Is that a problem?"

"Yes and no. I want to be with her, but I keep thinking of my wife, Annabelle. We were going to be together forever."

"How do you feel about this new young lady? What is her name?"

"Margo. She's smart and beautiful and twenty-three to my thirty-three. I don't care about the age difference. It doesn't bother her either.

I had a performance problem the first time we made love. I'm nervous it could happen again."

He pointed to his temple. "In my mind, I know Annabelle would want me to go on. In my heart, I still have feelings for her."

"Has the intimacy issue happened again?"

Edward felt hot under the collar talking to a woman about his sex life. "No. We've been great together, but I want a new beginning with this woman. I'm afraid I'll do something, or Margo will say something to trigger thoughts of Annabelle. I'm in a hell of a situation. In addition, she wants to be guardian to a little girl. I don't know if I'm ready to be a father figure. "

"What do you want?"

"I want to live again and give one hundred percent of myself to Margo and forget the past. It's holding me back."

He looked away. "It's hard for me to talk about intimacy with another female."

"I can recommend a male therapist, if you prefer."

Edward shook his head. "No, I'm making love to a woman so I might as well talk to one. I've never had a problem with sex. It's great between us now. However, lately Annabelle's face appears before me. I tense up. If I ever lose my erection again, Margo will leave me. Sometimes I think I don't deserve a life with someone new because I didn't do enough to keep Annabelle alive."

The doctor removed her glasses and sipped some water. "I think you should cut yourself some slack. The pressure you're placing on yourself is inhibiting you. Visualize yourself with Margo in a romantic setting and hold onto the mood it creates in your mind. Enjoy the pleasure of the physical contact. As to your deceased wife, I'm sure you did all you could. Regarding the child, if you love Margo, sharing in her affection for the girl will come with time. Let the child in gradually while you savor your lady's love. As far as performance, if Margo truly loves you that is the least of your problems."

Edward frowned. "You make it sound so simple."

Dr. Samson closed her notebook. "It isn't, but you need to slow things down. As I said, focus on getting to know Margo and take the time to find out who she is. Think of how good it feels to touch her and what you're looking forward to learning about her when you make love. I think it will lessen your anxiety and increase the pleasure for both of you. We're going to have to stop. Would you like to make another appointment?"

Edward looked in his pocket agenda. "The same time as today on Thursday? I'd like to talk more about how to put my relationship with Annabelle into perspective."

"Fine.

Dr. Samson opened her office door. "Life happens. First, focus on your relationship. Then, you can gain the child's confidence a little at a time. Children can sense when something is forced. Keep your eye on the prize—your lady."

Edward walked the rest of the way home. He recalled how natural it felt to hold Katya's hand the other day. He'd hoped to be a father when he and Annabelle married. Maybe it wasn't too late. He stopped into a bookstore and picked up a children's book about circuses for a future visit and an accompanying stuffed animal. He didn't think Katya had many toys, and every child needed a giraffe.

# Chapter Thirty

When Margo returned to the firm, her first priority of the day was to see Mr. Marshak. Her phone rang as she was about to walk down to his office.

"Margo, I need to speak to you about Mrs. Markova. Can I see you for a few minutes?"

"Absolutely. "

She grabbed a pad and was three quarters out the door when Nancy called.

"Hello?"

"It's me," Nancy said. "I had a fight with the new manager of the restaurant. He fired me. I was planning to quit. I'll be at your apartment tomorrow afternoon. My Uncle Vinnie owns a moving service. I've got everything under control."

"No Nancy. I want to pay my own way for this move. I'm out of it today. Katya's mother died. I'm on my way to see the head of the law firm."

"So sorry. I told my uncle about the kid. He has five of his own. See you tomorrow."

Margo walked into her boss's office with fear lodged in her heart.

She shuddered at what he would say, imagining Katya in a horrible situation.

He moved glasses up his nose and opened a thin folder. "Mrs. Markova made me promise not to say anything to you until there was no hope for her survival. She has appointed you as Katya's guardian."

Margo clasped her hands. "Thank God."

"Mrs. Markova signed a document to make you a standby guardian. You still have to go to the court and petition the judge for letters of guardianship. "

Margo listened intently, as though Katya's very existence depended on hearing every finite detail. "Does this mean I can't take care of her now?"

Marshak shook his head. "I'm afraid so. The standby guardian must go to court within sixty days and file a petition to have the guardianship approved and made permanent."

Margo could barely speak. So much had happened in the course of one summer. "I need to go to the Court to file that petition today because tomorrow afternoon I'm moving into my late uncle's apartment. You can deduct the hours from my paycheck."

Marshak shook his head and rose from his chair. "That won't be necessary,"

"I insist," Margo said. "I'd be lost without your guidance."

He grabbed his attaché case and stopped in the doorway. "Speak to Mary Ann. By the way, you have a lot of guts doing this at such a young age."

Margo told Mary Ann what she intended to do. "Leave now so you can get the paperwork out of the way and function here with a clear mind."

"No. I can leave at two and still make it. I owe you one."

Margo pushed herself to complete the day's priorities, skipping lunch and only interrupting her work flow to bring her mother up to date and tell her she'd be home late.

At two, she hurried down the block to the subway.

Running, she didn't see an empty soda can, tripped, and landed on her side. On all fours, she managed to right herself and walk down the stairs.

By the time she arrived at the Family Court, the line to file for guardianship was a mile long.

Her ankle and right hip where she'd fallen throbbed.

She shifted from one foot to the other.

At ten to four, she put her signature on the petition. Joyful, her bubble burst when the clerk told her that due to the upcoming start of the school year and holiday season, etc. etc. the judge was backlogged. Katya would be placed in a foster home until the paperwork was completed.

"When will that be?"

"In all probability, close to Christmas."

"What? I can't wait that long."

The clerk leaned across the desk. "Ms. Simmons, rules must be followed. However, I see on your application that you will be employed as a teacher as of next month."

She thumbed down further. "I also see you've asked for permission to tutor the child after school. Things will work out. Good day to you."

Margo had no choice. "Thank you for your time."

She limped out of the court with a lump in her throat and high anxiety. Life had handed her and Diana one hard knock after another.

Margo finally reached her office and hobbled down the hall to Mary Ann's office.

Mary Ann noticed the limp. "What happened to you?"

"I've been trying to do everything. It's caught up with me."

Mary Ann gave her the thumbs up. "I admire you for taking on motherhood to give the child a home filled with love."

"I wouldn't have it any other way. I hope you got my request to Mr. Marshak to take the extra time I've needed out of my paycheck."

"We'll talk about that at a later date when you don't have so much on your plate. Right now, finish up for the day."

Margo practically curtsied. "Yes."

~

BY THE TIME she returned to the Bronx, Margo's ankle from the side where she'd fallen was beginning to swell. In too much pain to hunt for her keys, she rang the doorbell.

Diana stared at the pained expression on Margo's face. "What happened to you?"

"I had a slight accident. Nancy will be here tomorrow afternoon to help with the move."

Her mother hurried into the kitchen and returned with an ice pack. "It looks a bit puffy. Shouldn't you have X-rays?"

"I don't have the energy, Mama. It will go away with time."

Margo sat in a recliner, lifted her feet onto a stool, and kept the ice on her ankle. She slept there, to keep her ankle elevated.

By morning, the swelling had gone down. It still hurt a bit when Margo applied pressure but all in all, it was a vast improvement over the previous day. Grateful, she looked skyward. *Please, give me a break.*

~

ON FRIDAY AFTER WORK, Nancy was waiting in the lobby of Uncle Harry's building with the movers. She pointed to Margo's ankle. "What happened to you?"

Margo frowned. "A freak fall."

"You'll sit and hand me the small boxes."

They took the service elevator to Uncle Harry's condo.

Nancy turned to Uncle Vinnie. "Can you send Alfonso and Lorenzo up?"

Within the blink of an eye, two strapping men were standing in the middle of the living room lifting boxes.

"I owe you one," Margo said.

Nancy shook her head. "No you don't. You're doing something wonderful for the kid."

~

It was so different to step into a doorman building. Entering a large lobby, Margo looked around at the white-and-gold tiled floor, upholstered couch in shades of beige and brown, and the oversized mirrors hanging on the walls.

"Wow, your uncle was one classy dude," Nancy said.

"I wish he were here. He'd like Edward and love Katya."

Nancy whispered low to Margo's ear. "So how's the sex going?"

Margo's cheeks turned red. "None of your business."

"I know that look. Truth time."

"I'm waiting for the other shoe to drop. I hope he goes to a therapist. Let's change the subject."

Margo expected to find an older bachelor's dust-covered apartment. To her relief, the only plastic was a garbage bag holding newspapers ready to be trashed. An Oriental rug covered a wide expanse of parquet floor in the dining room and a half-moon sofa rested under a bay window. Oil paintings covered the walls, and potted plants lined the windowsills. Margo made a note to buy a watering can. They looked kind of peaked.

Alfonso pointed to the boxes stacked in the hallway. "Where should we put these?"

"How about over there for now?" Margo replied, indicating a bare space behind a small china cabinet.

"Let's go into the bedroom," Nancy said. "I've never been in a bachelor pad like this."

To their disappointment, it was rather Spartan. A king-sized bed rested in the middle of a room with only a small television and several cassette holders in each corner.

Nancy opened the floor-to-ceiling closet. "Your uncle has a lot of suits."

Margo had to agree. To the left, row on row of shoeboxes were stacked up like soldiers. Suits of every color and material hung on thick rods. The inventory went on and on.

"I hate to disturb his belongings, but my clothes have to go somewhere."

"Don't be silly. Donate everything to the Salvation Army."

Nancy lifted a box tied with a pink ribbon and handed it to Margo. "I found this in the bottom of the closet. There's a card addressed to you."

Margo read the note.

To my darling niece,

Your aunt and I were never blessed. Please give this Shirley Temple doll to a special young lady. Hopefully, a child of your own.

Fondly,

Uncle Harry

She showed the message to Nancy. "Guys like your uncle no longer exist on this planet."

Margo's eyes misted over. "Your movers need to get to their next job. Let's roll faster."

A few hours later, the girls headed for the subway.

On the trip home, Margo nodded off until the car pulled into their station.

Her friend patted her shoulder. "We did well with the move. Go home and elevate that ankle."

Margo waved goodbye. "Thanks, Nancy. I'll settle up with you at Christmas."

WHEN HER ALARM clock went off on Saturday morning, Margo went back to bed for another hour.

A ringing cell phone intruded on her sleep at nine.

"Ice that ankle," Edward said.

"How did you know?"

"I called earlier, and your mother told me what's been happening. Rest. I'll call tomorrow to see how you feel. By the way, I got your text about Katya. Glad things are working out. "Margo was groggy but not so tired that she didn't pick up on the coolness in Edward's voice. If he wanted to be with her, he'd have to accept Katya as a part of her life.

Diana was waiting with an ice pack.

"Mama, you need to rest. I don't want you to tax your energy."

She pulled a letter out of her pocket. "This came yesterday. You've been so stressed; I didn't want to upset you."

Margo read her aunt's attorney's letter. She'd passed away, and the upstate cabin had been sold to pay off her debts.

She grabbed hold of her mother. "Please take care of yourself, Mama."

Diana smoothed Margo's furrowed brow. "Stop worrying. You'll give yourself a nervous breakdown. I have a ways to go but I'm getting stronger every day. I'll get dinner started."

Margo's cell phone rang.

"It's me," Edward said. "I was thinking. Labor Day is so hot in the city. What do you say we go to my friend's cabin upstate?

"It would have to be just an overnight. I have tons to do before I start the new job. Pick me up at seven so we can get a jump on the traffic."

"You've got it. Put down next Saturday on your calendar."

Margo had trouble focusing on her lesson plans wondering how Edwards's sessions with his therapist were progressing. Too soon to ask, but she was dying to know. From her limited experience, men didn't open up. They talked to guy friends or kept it locked inside.

# Chapter Thirty-One

Margo set up the condo and Katya's room in particular as best she could and tied up loose ends at the law firm.

By the time she saw Edward on Saturday morning, she was a bundle of nerves.

Once they were out of the city, Margo felt the muscles in her shoulders begin to relax.

Edward leaned over to kiss her cheek. "Sit back, honey, and enjoy the ride."

A short while later, she felt the car come to a halt at a roadside rest stop overlooking a panoramic view of Upstate New York Catskill Mountains.

"We there already?" Margo asked, rubbing her eyes.

"Not quite," he said. "I hope you brought a camera."

Margo turned on her digital and snapped nature in all of its emerald glory on trees. "I forgot how beautiful it is up here and hot in August."

"Ouch," she said, almost dropping her camera, which she'd attached to a mini-tripod.

"My ankle."

"My poor baby. I'll give you a healing massage when we get to the cabin."

AN HOUR LATER, he pulled into the driveway.

"I have the keys somewhere in here," he said, fishing around in his pocket. "Ah, here they are!"

Edward unlocked the door but allowed Margo to enter first.

"This place should be in Architectural Digest," Margo said, admiring the high-beamed ceiling and running brook. "It reminds me of pictures that I've seen of one of Frank Lloyd Wright's home, Falling Waters, in Pennsylvania."

Edward took her hand "Let's tend to that ankle."

Margo looked at the winding staircase leading to the upper level. "I don't think I can walk all of those steps."

Edward lifted her into his arms. "Problem solved."

He carried her into the master bedroom, laid her on the four-poster bed, and removed her sandals. "I wish you'd told me how much pain you were in."

Margo pulled him closer. "I needed to be with you."

"Don't move," he said, touching her lips with his finger. "The last time I was here I remember seeing massage oil in the medicine cabinet. My friend prepares for all contingencies."

Margo took off her jacket and waited.

He returned with a large bottle. "This should help."

He placed some in his hand and began to work it into her ankle.

"It's warm," Margo said.

"The swelling has gone down. Now you just need physical therapy."

"I couldn't have said it better myself."

Edward's rubbing heated up her entire body.

He lifted her shirt over her head.

She covered her bra with her hands.

"I have seen you naked."

He took off his jacket and shirt.

"Is it warm in here or just me?"

The rubbing was beginning to take effect.

His touch enthralled her.

Edward removed her jeans and placed hot kisses along her thighs and stomach.

Her skin sizzled.

Margo looked into Edward's eyes.

"Higher," she moaned.

Edward moved toward her breasts.

A few minutes later, they reversed positions.

"I don't want anyone to touch me but you. You know where all my pulse points are. Promise me it will always be this good," Margo said as Edward moved to her golden triangle.

Absorbed in their lovemaking, they lost track of time.

Several hours later, they held each other under tangled sheets.

"Let's stay here forever," she said.

"I have to fly to London soon. My manager has gotten his act together, and we're staffing up."

"I wish I could go with you."

"If you did, how would I get anything done? I think about you several times a day."

"Good thoughts, I hope."

"Good and naughty. I'll only be gone a week."

Edward nibbled on Margo's neck. "Reach into my jacket pocket. There's something in there for you."

Margo slipped out of bed and into his shirt.

"It's a bit late for that, isn't it?"

She blushed. "I'm shy."

She reached in his jacket and pulled out a box.

"Bring it over to me."

"Edward Master, what did you do?"

He pushed strands of hair off her face. "I bought a present for the woman in my life. Open it."

She stared at a pearl necklace with a diamond heart. "It's magnificent. I look at things like this in Tiffany's windows all the time. I never thought I'd own one."

He walked her over to a mirror. "Try it on."

Edward fastened it around her neck.

"I don't know what to say."

He kissed her neck and slipped the shirt off her shoulders.

"I like it better this way."

"You're irresistible."

By Sunday afternoon, Margo was tempted to stay the rest of the weekend. Then she thought of a much-needed paycheck until she was on the job a year and her inheritance kicked in.

As Edward locked up, she pushed back the door. "One more peek."

On the ride back to the city, Margo dreamed of a house she, Edward, and Katya could share as a happy family. If only her secret desires came true. Of all the things she wished for, this was the one she wanted most. However, there were still so many issues to overcome, not least of which Katya getting over her mourning period for her mother and seeing Margo in a different way—as a potential mother.

# Chapter Thirty-Two

On Monday night, Edward called from the airport. "Good luck tomorrow. We'll pick up where we left off when I return from London."

"Sounds good to me, but don't forget about Katya. Once I have guardian custody, you'll have to share me with her."

No response.

"Have to run. Love you."

ON TUESDAY MORNING, Margo had a nervous stomach. She tried to eat, but the food wouldn't stay down.

Her cell phone rang.

"Hello?"

"Ready for school?" Edward asked.

"I'm fine. Lesson plans, supplies, even visuals. Only one thing bothers me."

"What's that?"

"New teachers are always called in the end of August for an orientation. I assumed this would be the case for me. I didn't receive any calls or emails to this effect."

"Probably an oversight. Remember, own that classroom. You're in charge."

Margo looked at the time. "I'll give it my best shot."

Everything was so new in her life. She was use to the trip to Manhattan from the Bronx; she almost took the wrong subway to the school. She thought of a million things that could go wrong. Then she snapped out of her negative state of mind and reviewed her lesson plans. They were good. She'd make them work for the kids.

When the car pulled into her stop, Margo walked the two blocks to Park Elementary School, took a deep breath, and entered the building.

"So glad you're here. You'll be covering for a teacher on maternity leave," the principal said.

"I thought I was getting my own class."

"You are I'm just asking you fill in for the week. Around here we go with the flow, Ms. Simmons," the principal said.

Margo recalled Edward's advice—confidence. Okay, she didn't want to be a substitute teacher, but if it was a foot in the door, she'd use it as a stepping stone to bigger things.

"Is there anything I should know about the class?"

"They are third graders with a few English language problems and the rest are mainstreamed. I should have you in your class next week."

Margo dropped the folder into her attaché case and walked up two flights of stairs to the waiting students. She was starting to wonder if she would really be given a class of her own.

"Good morning, girls and boys. I'm Miss Simmons. I'll be your teacher for today. Third grade is my favorite.

She looked at the list the principal provided.

"I don't know your names. Would each person stand up when I call attendance?"

Once the formalities were over, Margo flipped through the seating chart on the permanent teacher's desk.

"Amelia, how would you like to be my helper for the day?"

"Oh yes."

Period by period, she got through the day.

At dismissal time, the kids asked if Margo would be returning.

"Of course."

~

AT TEN TO THREE, Margo returned her students to their parents waiting in front of the school. She checked the time on her I-Phone and left a message for Mary Ann. She'd promised to stop by the firm to proof-read a speech Mr. Marshak was giving to the bar association.

Disappointed in the way things had turned out, she shrugged her shoulders, wondering why she'd bothered to get a degree in education. The dream she'd had about being a teacher was gone. These weren't her kids. They were borrowed. She was keeping them nourished academically. The foot in the door was lodged in her mouth.

She put on her happy face as she headed for Katya's after-school program.

~

THE CHILD WAS SO happy to see Margo, she almost knocked her down.

"Ms. Margo, I thought you forgot about me."

"Never, sweetheart. I've been busy moving into my new apartment. Remember when I asked if you'd like to live with me?" Katya nodded.

"Well, I went to the court to ask permission."

No reaction.

"Unless you'd rather stay with your foster parents. I hope they're being good to my best girl."

"I like them. They have a poodle that I play with, but I miss you and Mr. Edward a lot. Could we all live together?"

Margo led her over to a table with two chairs. "Don't you think it's better if you and I get to know each other first? It's a big step for both of us."

"I guess so."

"How was the first day of school?"

"Okay, but I still don't speak English like the other kids."

"That's why I'm here, to help you practice."

"Will you come to see me every day?"

"As much as my jobs permit. I started teaching in a new school today, Remember I told you that I was also working at the law firm?"

"Oh, sorry. I forgot."

For the next hour, Margo listened to Katya read passages in her textbook and repeat phrases that were giving her trouble. At four thirty, Margo waited with the child until her foster mother came to pick her up.

She studied the woman. Neatly dressed, about late thirties with short cropped hair, and a bright smile.

"Hello," the woman said, extending her hand. "I'm Stephanie Packard. Katya has told me a lot about you. When she's not talking about Mrs. Markova, you're the main topic of conversation."

Katya spied her friend coming out of the school. "Can I play with Ava for a little while?"

"Sure, honey," Mrs. Packard said.

The woman leaned in to Margo. "I'm a bit concerned about Katya. Every night she lights candles in memory of her mother. That's fine. However, now she's having long conversations with her. Do you think I should speak to someone in addition to the school psychologist?"

Margo wanted to scoop the girl into her arms and carry her back to the condo.

"Might be a good idea. Children take death very hard. I know I did when my father died. Good to talk to you. Please watch over Katya. She's a special child."

Katya returned to Margo's side. "Can you have dinner with us?"

"I have to go back to work, but soon things will change. See you tomorrow. Keep up with your English studies, okay?"

Katya clung to Margo's waist. "I don't want you to go. Mama left me. Now, you're going."

Margo whispered in her ear. "I will be back tomorrow. Remember what I told you. I keep my promises."

IN THE CONDO Margo composed herself and called Diana. Overcome with disappointment about the temporary assignment and stressed over not being able to bring Katya back with her, she needed to hear the sound of her mother's voice.

"Hi, how did your first day on the job go?"

Margo cleared her throat. "I walked into school this morning expecting to have my own class. Instead, the principal told me to cover a maternity leave. When I spoke to her secretary

before I left, I was told the leave replacement backed out. They're cute kids, but I so wanted my own class."

"View it as a challenge. I'm sure you'll have your own next semester."

"I hope so, Mamma. I've worked so hard and come too far to settle now."

# Chapter Thirty-Three

Despite all her subtle hints to the principal and talks with the human resources department, Margo was no closer to having her own class. She was determined to finish out the semester, to be fair to the children, but stepped up her efforts to find a new school.

Her relationship with Edward wasn't doing well either. With him flying back and forth to London and Italy to set up new offices, an ocean kept them apart. Late in the evening, Margo jumped when the phone rang.

"How are you?" He sounded distant, like he was talking to a client.

"Swamped with papers to grade that the regular teacher didn't get around to doing and a load of other things. I'm sorry I never got to ask how your trip to London went."

"No worries. It was fine. I hope things go better for you. Are the children manageable?"

"Yes, that's the one saving grace. I'd like to continue this conversation, but I have to prepare for tomorrow."

"I'll catch up with you later in the week," Edward said.

At ten to midnight, Margo turned off the computer, dropped her lesson plans into an attaché case, and collapsed on the couch. To calm herself, she thought of making love to Edward. However, exhaustion superseded passion. She closed her eyes and drifted off.

The alarm woke her at five the following morning. Margo felt a stabbing pain in her lower back. It was her own fault for sleeping on the couch instead of her bed. Crap, on top of everything else, don't let this be my period. She stepped into the shower.

False alarm. However, she wouldn't be surprised if that was messed up too due to stress.

By Friday, the kids began to act up. She questioned why she put herself through the rigors of becoming a teacher only to wind up as a maternity leave replacement. From conversations she'd heard on break and at lunch, there was a pecking order and a preferred list, neither of which held her name.

Margo had to think of something positive before she went insane.

Her after-school work with Katya went well. The child was writing and speaking in full, grammatically correct sentences and her comprehension level shot up two levels.

Edward called as Margo was straightening up the classroom. "I know this is last minute, but how about catching a movie with me? I only have one day before I fly to London again. I need to see you."

"Okay, but this is dress down day. If you don't mind me in jeans and a T-shirt, I can come straight from work."

"Whatever you're wearing is fine. There's a romantic comedy playing at a movie theater on the West Side. I think you'll like the film."

"What time is the show?"

"Meet me in my lobby at four. There's a five thirty show. We'll grab a slice. You can fill me in on your week."

"Okay. I want to hear about your London progress."

Before turning out the classroom lights, Margo checked her makeup in a closet mirror. It was the only part of her she liked today. Maybe she should call Edward back and see a later movie to give her time to change into something more fashionable. No. If things were going to work out between them, he'd accept her as she was dressed right now.

When she arrived at the movie theater, Edward was pacing, as usual, in the lobby.

"Hi," he said, brushing his lips against hers. "It's good to see you."

"Same here."

Margo wasn't ready to give in to temptation, though the touch of his hand on her skin made it tingle. However, he went up and down the scale of emotions. She didn't want to crash and burn, again.

Edward bought their tickets. As they walked into the lobby, Margo noticed a photo booth. "I've always wanted to take a picture in one of those."

She pulled Edward over to the photo processor. "Come on. Let's have some fun."

Margo laughed as he tried to find a comfortable position on the small bench.

"This is a one-seater," Edward said, joining in her laughter. "I think I have a solution."

He pulled Margo onto his lap. "Better."

She placed her arms around his neck. "Say cheese."

Edward pressed the button and, a few minutes later, had three photos. "Not bad. You're the photogenic one."

Margo pointed to his ring finger. "You're not wearing your wedding band."

"I decided it was time to move on. That's why I'm seeing a therapist. I've had a few sessions with her."

"Margo's secret desires might come true. He cared enough about her to seek professional help. She had no need to doubt his love.

Edward rubbed the small of her back. "How badly do you want to see this movie?"

"Let's get out of here," Margo said.

"I was hoping you'd feel that way."

Edward handed the tickets to an elderly couple. "On the house. Enjoy."

The gentleman bowed. "Sir, you're a kind man."

Margo looked into Edward's eyes. "Where are we going?"

Edward hailed a cab. "To my place."

"Where to sir?" the cab driver asked.

"Sutton Place at Fifty Sixth Street."

On the way, Edward's hand moved along Margo's thigh.

When he went higher, she restrained him. "Patience."

The driver pulled up to the curb of Edward's townhouse. Inside the door away from prying eyes, he outlined her lips with his tongue.

"Welcome back." He said as he turned and unlocked the door.

Margo was still in awe of the crystal chandelier hovering over the foyer of his Sutton Place residence. "This place reminds me of a palace."

He ran his fingers over the smooth lines of a Lladró figurine of two lovers that was sitting on a table just inside the doorway. "People in love don't need palaces, Margo. I thought I told the housekeeper to store this piece." He picked it up and put it in the hall closet and Margo followed him into the den.

Edward locked the door to the den and lowered Margo onto a soft suede couch. "I can't wait to go upstairs."

He ripped off her jeans and kissed her silky skin as his lips traveled to her thong.

She held out her arms, gasping at the pleasures his touch would bring to her body. "Higher."

Margo removed his shirt and tie. She felt his heart beating faster. "I'm still crazy about this body."

"Same here."

She lifted her sweater over her head, anticipating the sensualities that awaited.

He tugged at her bra until he'd set her breasts free. Edward stripped off his pants.

Edward rubbed her nipples. He teased each one with his tongue and gentle bites until they became hard and firm to the touch.

He laid back on the sofa as she lowered herself on to him, aroused by what he would do to her naked body. Margo's body quivered as and slipped inside of her. She was so wet she needed no lubrication.

"Deeper," she pleaded.

He accommodated her by grabbing her ass and pulling himself deeper into her.

⌇

AFTER THREE HOURS of making love, Margo was starving. "How about ordering that pizza?"

Edward reached into his pants pocket for his phone. "What would you like?"

Margo stretched out on the couch. "Anchovies."

"He says delivery in about a half hour. Great, that gives us enough time for another round."

When the doorbell rang, Margo nudged Edward awake. "Honey, I'm starving. Please bring in our pizza. I don't want to move yet."

"I'm coming!" Edward shouted as he slipped into his pants. "I'll be right back."

She smiled. "I'll be right here."

Moments later Edward was back.

"Let's go into the kitchen and eat this before it gets cold, although nothing could get cold with you in the room."

The kitchen was the best part of the townhouse. "Uncle Harry's is nice, but I could do even more cooking here. So how's it going in London?"

Edward reached into a cabinet for plates and cutlery.

"I'm trying to set up operations, but my manager has conflicting ideas with the staff. I hope he settles in. He's the best negotiator in Europe, but a bit of a perfectionist."

"The farthest I've gotten is Toronto and one trip to Paris when I was five with Uncle Harry. I don't remember much."

"Patience, my dear. All good things take time."

Margo reached for the last slice. "Can we share? You make me ravenous."

"Did you know you have bedroom eyes and lips that must be kissed?"

"No one ever told me that before," Margo said, feeling like more of a woman than she ever had in her entire twenty-three years.

Her hand reached for the pizza. He pulled her into his lap and moved his hand under her shirt to her breast. "To touch you is to touch life. We can clean up later. Right now, there are more important things to do."

On the way back to the den, she pointed to a staircase. "Wouldn't it be better up there?"

Edward shook his head. "That's the past. Down here is the future."

He lifted her into his arms and lowered her onto the couch.

Edward stripped off his clothes, and removed Margo's thong.

His thrusts were slow and even. Margo became aroused as he nuzzled her nipples. The next thing she knew Edward was underneath her. Now, she was moving above him as he fondled her breasts.

"Yes," she screamed in ecstasy. "You feel so good. I want this moment to last as long as possible."

They cradled each other until he was back on top.

Edward's lovemaking was like trekking Mount Everest. The deeper he went, the more exhilarating the journey until she climaxed. "That was the first for me. No one has ever brought me to this moment."

An hour later, as they fell asleep in each other's arms, Margo stroked his arm and whispered, "I'm falling in love with you."

# Chapter Thirty-Four

While Margo showered, Edward made breakfast. A few minutes later, she came into the kitchen wearing Edward's robe and wrapped her arms around him.

"You were on fire last night," he said.

"I'm really very shy. You bring out the passion in me." Then she blushed. "I hope I haven't embarrassed you."

Edward drew her closer. "No, it's what I wanted from the first moment you walked into my office. Sex with you is like Christmas every day of the year. Each present gets better. "

Margo started to pull him out of the room. "You want to do it again?"

"Later. Let's eat first."

He lifted the lid on several dishes. "I didn't know how you liked them so I made several types of omelets."

Margo tasted the mushroom one. She then placed the eggs on a dish and walked to the table.

"How's the food?"

"Delicious," she said, nestling in Edward's lap.

"What are you doing about a new job? From our last conversation, I gathered that the present one isn't very rewarding."

"I have more experience now. I'm following up on some leads." Margo fed Edward a mouthful of eggs.

"How is Katya doing in the foster home? By the way it's hard to concentrate with your breasts rubbing against me."

"Am I tempting you? Here let me tie it closed so you can concentrate She's improving her English and looking forward to the day when she can move in with me as her guardian. I hope I find a new job soon because Uncle Harry only paid for a year's maintenance on the condo. I was speaking to some teaching friends. Looks like I'll need to set aside a budget for supplies. I want to give lots of handouts and make sure the desks are cleaned every morning."

Edward kissed her fingertips. "I've never met anyone like you, Margo. There's no challenge too big for you to take on."

"Maybe it's because nobody but Mom ever cared about me. I never bonded with my stepfather. Long story I'd rather leave alone for now. Let's do the dishes and clean up," she said. "I love this house. Each time I come here I see it from a different perspective. I want to make a good impression so I'll be invited back."

"No worries there," he said, pinching her bottom

With each step they took up the winding staircase, Edward remembered the last time he'd carried Annabelle out of their bedroom. The next day she died in his arms in the hospital. He promised himself he wouldn't think about it, but he still couldn't let go of her.

Midway, he turned around. "There's nothing to see up here. Let me show you my office. It's the best room in the house."

Margo tightened her hold of his neck. "Wherever you are makes me happy."

She followed him in. "Wow, look at all these history books. I could sit here for hours looking at that medieval tapestry."

He kissed the nape of her neck.

"I could spend hours doing foreplay, but I'm sure you have to prepare for your class. I'll drive you home."

Margo shook her head. There's a subway stop not too far from here."

"I'd feel better if you let me call you a cab, then."

Margo watched as he punched in numbers on his cell.

As she dressed, she heard him make the call.

"Triple D's Limousine Service? Great, she'll be outside in twenty minutes."

"The car will be here soon," he called out to Margo.

She hurried into her clothes. "I heard you."

While Margo towel dried her hair, Edward knocked on the bathroom door. "They're here."

"Coming."

Edward opened the front door and saw the disapproving look on Margo's face regarding the limousine.

"It's a long ride home. This is safer."

Edward opened the door and motioned for her to roll down the window. "Call me when you get home."

Margo tried to stifle her annoyance at the extravagance and turned to the driver. "Go."

"Yes, miss."

EDWARD RETURNED to his study and opened his online London file. He reviewed the notes the new manager had emailed the previous day. He was glad to see things had quieted down and the guy had developed a more cooperative mindset, but it hurt him the way Margo had left, angry, in the limousine. Annabelle had been in his life for so long. Maybe he wasn't capable of starting over, but he cared for Margo, enough to continue seeing the therapist.

He couldn't concentrate. He kept seeing the dejected look on Margo's face when he'd put her in the limo. He should've handled things better. He'd been dismissive without realizing it.

He locked up and walked over to Fifth Avenue and Tiffany's. A diamond pendant in the window caught his eye. He summoned the sales representative.

"I would like to see a piece in one of your window displays."

Edward held it up to the light. "It's stunning. Please gift wrap it."

"Of course, sir."

"Here you go, Mr. Master. I hope your lady enjoys this."

"Thank you."

Edward hadn't wanted to be with anyone this much since Annabelle. He had to stop screwing up and show Margo how much she meant to him.

On his way back home, he stopped into Victoria's Locker. Spotting a black lace bra and thong on a hanger, he felt a bulge in his pants, imagining how great Margo would look in them.

He texted her. What are you doing right now?

Finishing up the week's lessons.

You really turn me on. Wanted to assure you that I'm going to resolve my issues by talking them out with the therapist.

Margo leaped for joy as she read Edward's text. *Great because I need the closeness as well as the sex.*

Let's make plans for the Thanksgiving.

Aren't you rushing things a bit? It's not even Halloween. Besides, I can't spend all of the holiday with you.

Why not?

I asked Katya's foster mother for permission to take her to the Bronx Zoo. You could join us.

I have a better idea. Why don't we escape to an island—just the two of us?

Now who's being a kid? Once you get to know Katya better, you'll understand why I care about her.

Call Monday evening when you get home from work and let me know if you can get away for part of this weekend. I'll power up the engine on my BMW.

Margo didn't answer. She wondered if he'd ever understand about Katya and her need for companionship.

# Chapter Thirty-Five

Margo barricaded herself in the bedroom, forcing her mind to focus on her job search and not think about Edward. With his on and off the fence attitude about Katya, it was becoming easier to do. She had to have a win after two years of subbing and boxing shirts. She couldn't let her dream to be a teacher die. Her cell phone went off. Please don't let it be Edward.

She couldn't talk to him right now.

"How's everything?" Diana asked.

Margo closed the Internet. "Katya is doing well and has some new friends. That's the good part. The bad part is the principal lied to me. I was only filling in for the permanent teacher. I want a class of my own. I gave notice and asked for more hours at the firm. I'm searching job sites daily. I know they'd be happy to have me as a secretary at the firm—no way."

Margo heard Diana sigh. "When you were a little girl, I told you that I'd catch every raindrop so you'd always have sunshine. It hurts me to hear the down in your voice."

"I just want to get through tomorrow. Then, I'll sub and work at the firm until something comes along. I wish Uncle Harry hadn't set such strict conditions on my inheritance. I'd rather sell the condo and go back to living with you. I want to be positive, but right now the only good things in my life are you and Katya. Edward is still only a possibility."

MARGO'S last day at Park Elementary School was bittersweet. The kids made a card for her, but by the end of class, the principal watched as she gathered her supplies. She didn't wish her well or offer a reference. So much for all her good intentions.

The demands on her life were bringing tension headaches and insomnia.

A week and a half before Thanksgiving, she logged on to her email to read a message that a Madame Freses, headmistress at the East Side French School, wanted to see her for an interview. She replied immediately, making an appointment for the following Monday.

As she waited to be seen, Margo thought of a million things that could go wrong. Then she took stock of her life, did some yoga breaths, and when the headmistress approached, shook the woman's hand with confidence. She remembered what her favorite priest, Father James, had said to her. Do your best and let God do the rest.

"Good morning, Mademoiselle Simmons. So nice to meet you," the headmistress said, extending her hand. "I'm Madame Freses."

The petite, slim, elegantly dressed fifty-something woman escorted her into a large office. She opened a folder with Margo's name on the tab. "The best way for me to gauge your spoken knowledge is to converse."

"Of course. I'm ready when you are."

For more than an hour, the women talked about France, the school, and Margo's ideas on teaching. At the end, Margo's stomach was in knots at the thought of another rejection. She braced herself against the chair.

Madam Freses smiled. "You'll do well with my intermediate third grade. Shall we set a start date?"

Margo couldn't believe her ears. She'd gotten an offer without a lesson demo. She wondered what the catch was. "What would be good for you?"

"How about next Monday? It would be best if the students got to know you before the Thanksgiving recess, especially since a longer one follows at Christmas."

Margo wanted to shout out her enthusiasm. *Finally, a break.*

Madam Freses handed her a clipped packet of papers. "Since the semester has already begun, I've amended your contract to reflect salary adjustments."

Margo grabbed the headmistress's hands. "I won't let you down. Thank you so much."

Madam Freses smiled. "I'm sure you'll be a welcome addition to our staff."

Margo hurried out.

On the street, she called Edward. "I got the job."

"Fantastic, my love. I'm in a meeting now, but I want to hear everything."

Margo's heart did somersaults. Edward had never used the "L" word to her before.

She savored the moment. "I have to dash to the office."

She ended the call, but a few inches from the subway entrance, Margo's phone went off." "Sorry," Edward said. "I'm in the thick of things, as usual. How about we celebrate tonight over dinner at my place?"

"I thought you were busy."

"Only during the day. The night is for you. I'm being signaled. Have to go. Catch you later."

From the minute Margo walked into the firm she was deluged with paperwork. Mrs. Packard called at three o'clock to tell her the child had been hit in the head on the playground, she texted Edward.

I have to cancel our date. Katya had an accident. She's okay, but I have to hurry up to Bronx General Hospital.

Margo was surprised at Edward's response.

I'll meet you there.

WHEN SHE ARRIVED at the hospital, Katya was waiting with an icepack on her forehead.

Mrs. Packard approached. "She insisted that I call you."

"Thank you so much."

Edward had arrived a few minutes earlier.

The child held an American Girl doll in her lap.

"Look what Mr. Master brought me. Isn't she pretty?"

Margo kissed the child's bruised forehead. "Yes. Does it hurt a lot?"

"A little bit, but the nurse fixed it."

She pulled Edward aside. "You're amazing."

"My secretary has a grandchild. She did me a favor."

The attending doctor walked over to Margo and Katya's foster mother.

"Are there any follow up instructions?"

The doctor handed them a printed form. While Mrs. Packard signed the release papers, Edward called Roger to bring the car around to the front of the hospital.

ON THE WAY HOME, Katya talked about her favorite flavor of ice cream, how much she wanted to live with Margo, and what a nice man Mr. Master was.

A short while later, as Mrs. Packard looked on; Edward lifted Katya into his arms and rested the sleeping child on the bed in her room.

Margo said a brief goodbye to Edward and returned to the office to finish out her day. She dragged her tired body back to the condo and relieved that Katya was okay, turned on her computer to check for

French lesson plans. True to her word, Mrs. Freses sent her the curriculum for the rest of the year. Margo was on her way.

~

LATER IN THE EVENING, her cell phone rang. "I'm sorry for the way I acted. I was being selfish."

Margo nodded. "I agree."

Edward continued. "I wanted to talk to you about the child. Are you sure you're not taking on too much responsibility petitioning to be her guardian?"

"We've discussed this already."

"I worry about you. Running in so many directions. It's not good for your health or us."

"I'm used to it," Margo said.

"I have to fly to Tokyo. We got a great deal on office space. When I come back, why don't we have Thanksgiving at the townhouse? There's more room. If her foster mother will allow her to come, I think Katya and your mother would enjoy my place."

"Sounds like a plan.

"I know teaching is important to you. I'll bring back presents for Katya."

"The most important thing is to bring yourself."

Margo really cared for Edward but wondered when he would realize that heartfelt feelings were more important than store bought gifts.

# Chapter Thirty-Six

At four o'clock the next morning, Margo woke up with a tension headache. Reaching for Tylenol in the medicine cabinet, she thought of something her mother had told her when she was in grammar school. Anything worthwhile takes patience and perseverance. She bent down on her knees and prayed that the twenty young souls waiting for her to teach them in a few hours at the French school would be patient with her.

Margo shuttled over to the East Side and walked into the school with butterflies in her stomach.

"Bonjour, Ms. Simmons. I'll take you to your class," the headmistress said.

Margo recalled Franklin Roosevelt's great line about having nothing to fear but fear itself. However, two steps from entering the classroom her mind raced. Maybe they wouldn't like her.

She followed the headmistress into the classroom.

"Bonjour, students. I want you to welcome your new teacher, Ms. Simmons. As we discussed, please work together as a team."

One by one, each student walked up to Margo and handed her a greeting card. "Bienvenue. Welcome."

For the rest of the week and all the way to Thanksgiving, Margo walked on air. The students flourished under her tutelage. It also helped to be teaching in an immaculate classroom stocked with supplies and plenty of books as well as a Smartboard that worked. However, Margo was too tired at night after assessments and grading papers to do more than make a quick call to Katya say hello. As to Edward, his long-distance calls went unanswered as Margo struggled to keep up with testing and the demands of parents willing to pay premium tuition for their children.

Margo's euphoric bubble burst when Katya's foster mother left a message that the holiday was a family affair. She could see the child for the circus outing she'd mention on Sunday afternoon of the holiday weekend.

When Edward returned from his overseas trip and heard what had happened, Margo was surprised, again, at his response. "The child needs stability. She's still in mourning for her birth mother."

"I know, but I was so looking forward to our first holiday dinner together." Margo said.

She heard him flipping pages. "I offer this suggestion. Since her foster mother was amenable to a Sunday outing, we take the girl to the circus. This way the holiday ends on an upbeat note for both of you."

Margo couldn't argue with that logic. "Fine, I'll make the arrangements, but what about tickets. They'll be hard to get the last minute."

"I already bought them, remember?"

"Sorry. I have a lot on my plate these days."

"As you tell the kids, chill Margo."

"I'll meet you at the box office of the circus on Sunday. Until then, try to relax."

MARGO STOOD with Katya watching as Edward walked up.

"Good morning ladies. Are we all set for today's main event?" Edward asked as he leaned down to Katya.

"Oh yes, Mr. Edward. I can't wait."

Soon they were seated in comfortable box seats up close to the action.

When the lights dimmed in the circus tent, Margo smiled as Katya held her breath in anticipation of what was to come.

The ringmaster entered and shouted: "Is everyone ready for the greatest show on earth?"

"Yeah!" the kids shouted back.

"During our intermission, children will be able to ride the ponies participating in today's show."

Katya turned to Margo. "Can we please?"

"Sure."

"This is my first time at the circus," Katya said.

"We're going to make it special for you, right, Edward?"

"Absolutely."

They watched as Katya sat mesmerized by the performers.

During intermission, Katya looked up at Edward. "Can I have a pony ride now?"

He held out his hand. "Let's go."

The joyful expression on Katya's face as a member of the circus staff led her pony around the ring made the trip worthwhile to Margo. She took pictures, which helped take her mind off the pain in her ankle that was still swollen.

On the ride to the Packard home to the Bronx, Katya fell asleep in Edward's arms.

Mrs. Packard opened the door and greeted them. "Hello, did everyone have a good time?"

The child lifted a bag of toys. "Look, there's even a giraffe."

Back in the limo it was Margo's turn to go home. Edward walked Margo to the door. "Here's where we say goodnight."

"Between our hectic schedules, there doesn't seem to be time for us anymore," Margo said.

He cupped her face in his hands. "We'll talk more when I get back from Tokyo."

～

A FEW DAYS before the holiday break, Madam Freses asked Margo to bring some papers to the boardroom. That's when she saw the plaque. Moving closer, she read the inscription.

The East Side French School is honored to announce the appointment of Monsieur Edward Master as a board member. He follows in the footsteps of his grandfather, Malcolm, without whose generous endowment this school would not exist.

Margo's eyes rolled. She lost her balance and nearly hit her head against the wall.

It appeared that her job offer was Edward's handiwork. Don't lose your cool. You're in public. Finish out the day and give Edward a piece of your mind at home.

WHEN MARGO RETURNED to the apartment, she called Diana.

"Can you imagine what Edward did?"

"You've been struggling on your own for so long. There's no harm in a helping hand. Furthermore, you don't even know for certain that he was involved. Just because you saw a plaque with his grandfather's name on it doesn't mean that he did anything special for you. Did you ever stop to think that maybe your background sealed the deal?"

Margo had inherited her father's suspicious nature. Perhaps Mama was right. However, she'd prefer to hear the truth from Edward.

"Okay, I'm going to call him now and find out what happened, but be prepared for a Christmas with just the two of us. We discussed bringing Katya to the townhouse and getting a tree, but now, I don't know."

"Fine, dear, whatever you decide."

Margo took a chance calling Edward. He hadn't given her the exact date of his return, only saying before Christmas.

"Hi, just walked in the door and missing you."

Margo had planned to be cool, but she blurted it out. "Did you ask Mrs. Freses to give me a gifted and talented class and did she do it because of your grandfather's endowment?"

"No and yes. I've known Madam Freses for many years. I did have a conversation with her but only after she called to ask if I'd be pledging my usual sum. She mentioned she had hired a new teacher and I told her I hoped her talents would be put to the best possible use. I had nothing to do with her decision to hire you; she came to that conclusion entirely on your merits and ability."

Margo exhaled for the first time in hours. "Total truth?"

"If you were here now, you'd see me raising my right hand."

"Okay, I believe you, but I think we need a break."

"We hardly see each other now."

"If we're meant to be, it will hold until Christmas."

"Then, I guess I'll extend my trip to London. Would you ride with me to the airport?"

"Yes."

❧

IN THE BACK of the limousine on the way to John F. Kennedy International Airport, Edward lifted an envelope out of his jacket pocket. "Open it."

Margo rolled her eyes as she stared at a confirmation of arrival for two people to The Fairmount Hotel in Bermuda for the Christmas holiday.

He nibbled on her ear. "Soon, enough, my luv, we'll be walking on pink sand in Bermuda and lying naked in each other's arms."

Margo looked at the dates. "This was a lovely gesture, but I wish you'd spoken to me first. Katya is looking forward to presents under the tree, hot cocoa, and me. Her foster mother is bringing her over on Christmas Eve."

She crossed her fingers. "I've completed my ninety days of training. I received word from the judge a few days ago that my petition to be her guardian should be finalized in a few days. Maybe we can get away later in the week."

Edward kissed her fingertips. "As long as we have some alone time together. Come with me as far as the Security Screening area."

Margo would walk the length of the airport if he continued to be this understanding about her need to spend time with Katya.

When Edward's flight was called, he turned to her. "I have something special for you when we celebrate Christmas. However, I prefer to give it to you in Bermuda."

"Sure, whatever." Margo hadn't a clue as to what she'd give him. It was hard to buy a present for a man who'd tasted of every aspect of life.

She grabbed hold of his broad shoulders and whispered in his ear, "I'll miss you."

BACK IN THE APARTMENT, Margo had a heart to heart conversation with Diana. "What if Edward isn't serious about me? I couldn't take it, Mama. I had a raw deal with Sergio. One disastrous relationship in a lifetime is enough."

"Stop predicting doom and gloom," Diana advised. "I'm the last one to preach on successful marriages with the way things turned out for me and Jerry, but all indications are Edward really cares for and about you."

Margo bit down hard on a carrot stick. "Katya and I are a package deal, Momma. Edward can't have one without the other."

"Only time will tell, my dear. Give it that time."

The next day when Margo returned home, a basket of cheeses, crackers, and wines waited for her with the Concierge. The card was addressed to her and Katya.

*I passed a store catering to Parisian tastes and pallets. Hope you enjoy the goodies. Look underneath. I added something special for you and the girls.*

Margo pressed her hand to the bottom of the basket. "Oh, how wonderful."

Three bottles of the latest Parisian scents in bubble wrap. "How thoughtful. "

Margo lifted a parchment paper out of an envelope.

*Darling, I have something else for you, but you'll have to wait until I return. It's not the kind of gift I want your mother or the little one to see, but I hope it will give you pleasure to wear it and me to appreciate you in it.*

> *Edward*

She dropped the paper into her attaché case. All this talk about skimpy lingerie was making her think twice about the forever after part of their relationship. Edward was a great lover, but she feared he'd forgotten what it meant to be a partner.

# Chapter Thirty-Seven

By the third week in December, Margo deposited her paychecks into her savings account. She allowed herself enough money for lunch and a present for Katya The only gift she could afford to give Edward was affection, but she hoped he'd continue to treasure their relationship as well.

At midnight two days before the holiday while she slumbered, Margo's cell phone went off.

"Hello Margo, my flight landed at JFK. I can't wait to see you."

"Edward?"

Margo rubbed her eyes and looked at the clock. "I haven't heard from you in two weeks. Is everything alright?"

"I've been working nonstop."

"Tell me about it. End of the year school responsibilities plus I had to do some overtime on Monday so Mary Ann could take off. I owed her. She's been good to me."

"That's my girl always helping someone. Rest up. I plan on ravaging you with kisses and doing naughty things when we go to Bermuda."

"We'll talk when I see you."

Whatever happened, Margo made up her mind to focus on Katya

and holding on to her job. She was getting the uncomfortable feeling that Edward's desires didn't include commitment. She looked forward to quality time with the child on Christmas Eve, even if it meant sharing her with foster parents, for one last time.

"I'LL GET IT," Katya said, running to answer the door. "Mr. Edward! Happy Christmas Eve. We missed you a lot," she said.

He scooped her into his arms and dangled a shopping bag. Hello, princess for you, presents from around the world."

She turned to Margo. "Do I have to wait until Christmas to open them?"

"Don't you think we should wait until Grandmother Diana gets here?"

"Okay."

During dinner Katya fired off a myriad of questions, which Edward answered in rapid succession. As soon as they finished the meal, the child began to yawn.

"I think someone is getting tired," Margo said.

When Katya and her foster parents had left the condo, Diana said her goodnight as well.

She pulled Margo aside. "Remember what I said."

Margo cleared the table and filled the dishwasher. A few minutes later, she felt

Edward's arms around her.

"I've missed you so much."

He carried Margo into the bedroom. "Don't move. I'll be right back."

Edward returned with a lavender shopping bag. "I think you'll find everything you need in there for our overdue reunion."

Margo lifted a bottle of perfume called Temptress along with a negligee with only enough lace to cover her important parts. She blushed. "It's nice of you to think of me."

"Why don't you get ready?"

Margo tiptoed into the bathroom. Edward had seen her naked before, but this negligee made her feel cheap. Maybe the perfume would compensate. Opening the heart-shaped bottle, she removed the stopper and took a whiff. Too sweet. If she had the salesgirl who'd sold Edward this junk, which probably cost a fortune, she'd strangle her. Tempted to shower and slip into her own nighty, Margo thought of the trouble Edward had gone to for her. He was a man, what did he know. She covered herself with her uncle's flannel robe and walked back into the bedroom.

"Our first Christmas together."

Margo jumped as he popped the cork on a bottle of champagne and poured the bubbly liquid into two glasses.

"To us, darling," he said, placing one in her hand.

"How about to the three of us?"

"Of course."

Margo sat beside him.

"I'd rather see the creation I bought for you."

"I'm shy."

"Maybe you need a little loving to get things under way."

As his lips traveled down Margo's neck, she was surprised at her reaction. Something didn't feel right. "I'll be back in a flash."

Margo wet a washcloth and swabbed the spots containing the most perfume. Stepping out of the flimsy lace, she pulled on a midnight blue nighty and returned to Edward.

"What was that all about?"

"If you want to make love to me, you'll have to accept me as I look right now."

"I thought you'd be overjoyed with sexy lingerie from Europe."

"Edward, everything doesn't have to have a designer label and an expensive price tag. You're making love to me, not the lace."

His arms surrounded her. "You're absolutely right. It won't happen again. You're the main event, not the trimmings."

∽

Two days after Christmas, Margo and Edward waited at the airport for their flight to Bermuda. She'd given emergency numbers to Diana but still felt guilty about not spending more time with Katya over the holidays.

Their flight was called. Margo started to walk toward the economy section.

"Where are you going?" Edward asked.

"To our seats."

Edward pointed to First Class.

"We're right here."

As they settled in, Margo looked around the spacious area. "It's like the veranda in your townhouse."

A few minutes before takeoff, a flight attendant came around with champagne and hors d'oeuvres. Once they were in the air, a full menu of food and amenities were given to all of the First Class passengers. "I could get used to this."

Edward smiled. "I hope so."

Margo took some deep yoga breaths. "I'm unaccustomed to luxurious living and tantalizing treats. It will pass, I guess."

Edward tightened her seatbelt. "This is only the beginning."

Too excited to focus on her surroundings, Margo ate her dinner with gusto and, as the featured movie came on, fell fast asleep.

A few hours later, Edward shook her hand. "We're here."

She raised the window shade and looked out at the islands of Bermuda.

A quick walk through Customs and Immigration and out to a waiting limo for the ride to the Fairmont.

"Since this is your first time to the island, I thought you'd prefer to be in the center of everything. I think you'll like the Fairmount. It's an outstanding hotel."

Margo put her head on Edward's shoulder. "Those recliners were great, but right now, all I want is a shower. I feel grungy."

He let go of a mischievous smile. "Soon, you'll be enjoying a variety of activities."

Margo popped off a few shots of the sculptured contours of the island and the unusual design of the homes.

"Edward why do the building roofs look like that?"

"Well hon that's because Bermuda is short of fresh water and therefore every drop of rain on the roofs is impounded and stored in cisterns. Ah, we have arrived.

"Welcome, back, Mr. Master," the concierge said. "Always a pleasure to see you and of course your guest."

Edward nodded. "It's been too long, Reginald." He turned to Margo. "This is my special friend, Ms. Simmons."

Reginald bowed. "A pleasure."

Within seconds of ringing a small desk bell, they were taken to the penthouse suite.

"I think you'll find this to your satisfaction," Reginald said.

Margo opened the terrace doors and looked out onto the ocean. "Edward, come here."

She pointed to the beach. "The sand really is pink."

He tipped Reginald and nibbled on her lower lip. "Let's go for a swim."

~

As they floated on the sapphire waves, Edward reached for Margo. "Happy?"

"Yes. I can't remember when I've been so mellow. I wish we could do this every month."

He lifted her into the air. "One day with our own little one."

Margo put some distance between them. "What's Katya?"

Edward swam to her. "You know what I mean."

Margo looked around. "Let's shower and see what's for dinner. I hear the restaurants here are a feast for the eyes as well as the pallet."

Edward massaged her shoulders. "As long as we can pick up where we left off later."

~

BACK IN THE PENTHOUSE, he led Margo into a huge bathroom in which a heart-shaped Jacuzzi built for two took center stage. "Let's make up for lost time." Edward turned on the jets and held out his hand.

Margo gripped it to steady her descent into the bubbling water. "Heaven. I may not come out until morning."

For the rest of the week, Edward and Margo only left each other's side to change for dinner, but by the thirtieth of December, Edward tired of nonstop talk about Katya.

"What's wrong?"

"I went to a lot of trouble to arrange this trip. All you've talked about is Katya. I sometimes think she's on your mind when we make love. Remember me? The guy who's in love with you."

"If you feel that way, there's no point in us staying here any longer."

Edward watched Margo arrange for a flight back to New York. She covered the receiver. "Can you be ready in an hour?"

"Yes."

❧

ON THE WAY to the airport, Margo had a change of attitude. She reached out for his hand. "I'll make it up to you. At least we had a few days in Bermuda."

The look of disappointment on Edward's face stabbed at her heart. "I was planning something very special for us." A smile slipped off Margo's lips. "This isn't a business deal, Edward."

From the moment they took their first class seats at the airport until their flight landed in New York City, Margo's heart, soul, and mind were not on Edward.

❧

IN THE LIMO on the way to her apartment, Margo couldn't find a comfortable spot.

"Do you have any Tylenol? I forgot to pack it."

210

"I never touch the stuff. When I'm tense, I work out." Edward's stiff upper lip wasn't helping.

Margo wondered where the empathy he'd shown earlier in the relationship had gone.

When Roger pulled curbside to her condo building, she jumped out and hurried up to her apartment.

Edward took a ticket out of his jacket pocket, asked the Concierge for an envelope, and wrote Margo's name on the front. "Can you see that Ms. Simmons gets this?"

"Yes, sir."

~

AT A MINUTE to midnight as Mrs. Lopez and Diana Simmons prepared to toast the New Year with eggnog, Edward kissed Margo under the mistletoe at the St. Regis Hotel ballroom.

In their suite a few hours later, he opened a velvet box from Tiffany's and slipped a four-carat solitaire diamond onto her finger.

Margo couldn't breathe. The room spun around.

She fell into his arms. "Edward, what's this all about?"

"I want you to live with me. Down the road, when it's right for both of us, we'll take things to the next level."

Margo was crushed.

He hadn't mentioned Katya. This proposal didn't sit right with her.

She rested the ring in the palm of his hand. "I don't think so."

Edward stared into her teary eyes but gave her no response.

"Goodbye, Edward."

Margo grabbed her things and waded through a sea of revelers in the lobby to catch a cab back to her apartment.

~

EARLY THE NEXT MORNING, Nancy called Margo.

"Hi, Happy New Year. I haven't heard from you in a while. Is everything okay with you and Edward?"

"We broke up. He wanted me to move in with him. He didn't even mention Katya."

"Get real, honey. Edward is a wealthy, powerful man. I'm sure he has other things in mind. Be patient. Don't let this catch off the hook."

"No. It's over."

# Chapter Thirty-Eight

Edward was out of her life but as of January, Margo had been appointed Katya's guardian. Happiness bloomed in the Simmons household.

As spring replaced a blistery, bitter winter, the headmistress at the French School told Margo her contract would be renewed. The parents were so pleased with her teaching abilities they told their friends, increasing the enrollment by five percent. Her cell phone went off as she finished grading papers at school.

"Hello Mr. Steinberg, I haven't heard from you for a while. I was beginning to think you'd forgotten about me."

"Never my dear girl. I received the copy of the contract renewal for the next school year that you sent to me. I have good news. The terms of your uncle's will have been met. You can rightfully claim your inheritance. I spoke to your mother the other day. She'll be coming in to sign the divorce papers."

Margo was only sad that her mother tolerated Jerry's antics for long. "She told me. Thanks so much for all of your help."

"Carry on, dear girl. You're doing beautifully."

"Thanks. I hope the next thing I ask for advice on is a children's book I'm writing. I'll need a good lawyer to look over the contract."

"You can count on me."

Margo hung up with mixed emotions. She'd be able to pay off her student loans but felt sad for Diana's situation, which mirrored her own failed love life.

A ringing telephone interrupted thoughts about Good Friday dinner.

"Hi, Mom. I have to put in another hour at the law firm. Are you too busy at the shop to come over to the apartment later on?"

"No worries. It's about time someone turned your new place into a proper home. The way you've been running ragged, it's a wonder you get as much done as you do. Sorry I've been absent mentally sorting through the divorce mess. How are you doing?"

"Okay, under the circumstances. It will take a long time to heal, but for Katya's sake, I'm making an effort. However, the next time I won't let a man into my heart until I can see into his soul."

"Dream on, my dear. My mother used to say men are like cats. You never know where they're going to land. It also applies to their hearts. They do a darn good job of camouflaging them."

"Amen to that."

THE NEXT DAY, Margo's first task was to drop off material for one of the firm's preferred clients. He was waiting for her in the boardroom.

"Thanks, Margo. Sorry to make you a messenger, but Mr. Master is in a bit of a rush. He needs to return to London and papers must be signed," Mr. Marshak said. Margo looked straight ahead, pretending that Edward wasn't in the room.

Except for the puffy eyelids, he hadn't changed a bit. In fact, he was handsomer than Margo remembered.

"How are you?"

"Fine."

Mr.Marshak handed him a pen.

"How are Katya and your mother?" Edward asked, not looking up.

"Great."

Margo had to get out of there before her heart burst. "If you'll excuse me, I have a lot to do before I leave."

"I better get going as well," Mr. Marshak said. "Look over all of the documents. Call me the next time you're in town."

Edward frowned. "That won't be for a while."

"Whatever," Marshak replied and was gone.

Edward turned to Margo. "Can we talk for a minute?"

She took a seat at the oblong oak table.

Edward moved his chair closer. "I never meant to hurt you."

"I don't want to discuss my private life in the workplace."

Edward reached for her hand. "I agree. What are you doing for dinner tonight?"

"Spending it with Katya, of course."

"I want to clear the decks before I return to London. I'll be here through Sunday. Would you and Katya join me for a belated Easter dinner?"

She shook her head. "I don't think so. The girl has been through enough emotional pain. She's a happy, well-adjusted child now. I want it to stay that way."

"Then, how about you joining me for dinner?"

"I don't think that's a good idea." Margo rose from her seat. "I have to go."

For the rest of the day and on the subway ride home and throughout dinner, Margo couldn't stop thinking about Edward. When Katya left the table, Margo called Diana.

"Good for you," her mother said. "The man has nerve. Leaves for London and then wants to waltz back into your life as though nothing happened."

"Mama, I couldn't agree more, but I'm still in love with him."

"Someone more deserving of your love will come into your life."

Between Katya and work, these days Margo only wanted to see the lining of her eyeballs.

When the phone rang at ten thirty, she barely had the energy to lift it to her ear.

"I never stopped loving you," Edward pleaded. "Please give me another chance. I can change. I started by selling the house. It's part of my past. You're both my future. I've picked up where I left off with the therapist."

"I thought you were moving to London."

"So did I until I saw you again."

"I'm sorry, but you ripped out my heart once. I can't go through that again."

She hung up.

~

AN HOUR LATER, Edward tried again. "I don't want to lose you."

"If you promise to stop calling me, I'll meet you tomorrow for brunch."

"Eleven thirty at The Park. It's a new place. I think you'll like it."

"Whatever, goodnight."

~

EDWARD LEAFED through half a dozen magazines while waiting for the therapist to see him.

"Good evening, Edward."

"I hate phone sessions. I've been setting up an office in London, Dr. Samson. My work there is done. "

"What do you want now?"

Edward squeezed a stress ball in his right hand. "To make a life with Margo and Katya, if they'll have me. I've had time to think about what I said to her last New Year's Eve. It was wrong of me to ask for a live-in arrangement."

Dr. Samson jotted down notes.

"I've had time to reflect on everything in my life. I want Margo and Katya with me. They're my reason for being alive."

Dr. Samson shook her head. "A child may be a smaller human being but still requires love and attention. You've told me. Now tell them."

"I'm going to propose marriage to Margo. I hope she'll give me another chance. I'm ready for forever. I didn't think I'd ever say the words will you marry me again and mean it, but if I lose her and the girl, I've lost everything."

Dr. Samson stood up. "Well then, Edward. I think you should practice how you are going to say it until you get your words perfect."

He extended his hand. "Thanks, Dr. Samson. It's been a pleasure to know you."

She shook her head. "I wish you well, but remember it takes two to make a relationship work. Give it your all. It sounds to me like the young lady and her daughter are worth it."

Edward smiled. "They are."

~

MARGO THOUGHT about all that had happened as she walked to a crosstown bus.

She couldn't hear anymore lies. Through teary eyes, she called Edward.

"Hi. Why the call? You'll be seeing me in a few minutes."

"I can't do this. I hope your London venture is a big success. Good-bye, Edward."

Margo retraced her steps back to the condo and waited for Katya to come home from a play date with her new classmate, Chrystelle.

For the rest of the semester, she buried herself in her work and poured all of her extra time and love into the child.

~

A WEEK LATER, Diana called to ask her to go with her to Mr. Steinberg's office. Something about Jerry complaining about the terms of the divorce.

Margo asked Mrs. Lopez to babysit.

On her way, Margo got a message from Diana to meet her in the lobby of Edward's building. Since he was now in London, there was no threat to her heart or mind. No more empty promises from a man who couldn't commit. When she arrived, Diana was there with Katya.

"What's going on?"

Diana pressed in on the elevator button.

The three girls stepped inside.

"Edward has been calling me nonstop. At first, I hung up on him.

Then, I started to listen. He really cares about you and Katya. I know a cad when I see one. That's not Edward. Hear him out. Then, you're free to leave.

They walked up to the receptionist. "Mr. Master is expecting you. I'll tell him you're here."

WHILE DIANA and Katya looked on, Edward bent down on one knee in his office and took Margo's hand.

"I thought this was the perfect place since it's where we first met. Would you do me the honor of becoming my wife?"

Margo went weak in the knees.

Edward lifted a small ring box out of his pocket and opened the lid.

"Oh, how beautiful," Katya said.

Margo looked up at him with tears of joy in her eyes. "This time, I do believe you're ready for a relationship. Let's start with that, okay?"

Edward smiled. "Yes."

# Discussion Questions

1. How does Margot's home life affect her outside relationships?

2. Would Edward and Margo fit the expression love at first sight?
If so, how? Is love at first sight possible?

3. Margot has a full life—job search, new condo, tutoring of Katya.
Is Edward an intrusion?

If yes, why? If not, how does he affect these areas as they form a relationship?

4. Is Margo truly trying to give Katya all that she missed out on in her own fractured childhood?

5. Aside from physical attraction, what other elements make a relationship work?

Are they present with Edward and Margo?

# About the Author

J.L. Regen's book was inspired by a real life story of lovers who join hearts despite many obstacles. J.L. lives in the New York metropolitan region, is a published photojournalist, and has short suspense stories online. This is J.L.'s first contemporary romance.

J. L. has also published three nonfiction books. J.L. would love to hear from you. Email comments writerjr1044@gmail.com or visit her at JOANSBOOKSHELF.COM